Readers Love ANDREW GREY

Buck Me

"The setting is well-done and the characters realistic. The author puts me right there, on the ranch, with Emmet."

—Sparkling Book Reviews

Lost and Found

"The next time I get an Andrew Grey book I will definitely not start reading it at 12:00 AM because once I start one of his books, I can't put it down and the next thing I knew it was 5:00 AM but it was worth it."

—Paranormal Romance Guild

Second Go-Round

"I would absolutely recommend this book, especially for Andrew Grey fans. It stays true to his easygoing style of writing and will make you feel things."

—Love Bytes Reviews

Half a Cowboy

"Mr. Grey has such talent in using language, rather than simplistic action, to establish [characters'] feelings for each other."

—Rainbow Book Reviews

Hard Road Back

"As short as the book is, this felt like a slow burn to me, which I loved. This book has two of my favorite tropes, friends to lovers and the bed-sharing thing…need I say more?"

—The Blogger Girls

By Andrew Grey

Published by Dreamspinner Press
www.dreamspinnerpress.com

By ANDREW GREY (cont'd)

Published by DREAMSPINNER PRESS
www.dreamspinnerpress.com

By ANDREW GREY (cont'd)

Published by DREAMSPINNER PRESS
www.dreamspinnerpress.com

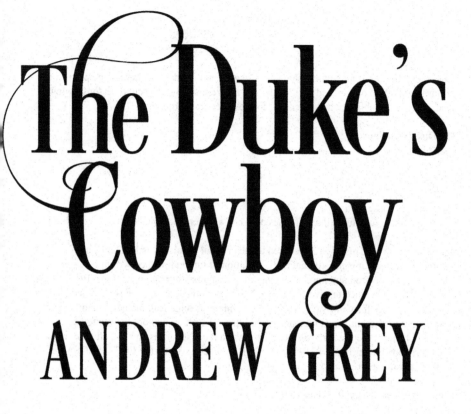

The Duke's Cowboy

ANDREW GREY

DREAMSPINNER
PRESS

Published by
DREAMSPINNER PRESS

8219 Woodville Hwy #1245
Woodville, FL 32362 USA
www.dreamspinnerpress.com

The Duke's Cowboy
© 2024 Andrew Grey

Cover Art
© 2024 L.C. Chase
http://www.lcchase.com
Cover content is for illustrative purposes only and any person depicted on the cover is a model.

Trade Paperback ISBN: 978-1-64108-415-4
Digital ISBN: 978-1-64108-414-7
Trade Paperback published March 2024
v. 1.0

CHAPTER 1

THE BACK tires slid again, kicking the old truck out to the side. Damn and blast. George should have paid more attention to the tires when he'd bought the thing in Cheyenne.

He was in real trouble. The snow was getting heavier and the highway more dangerous. The roads would only become worse the longer he was out. He knew the highway was probably in better shape than the surface roads, but he'd still prefer to find an exit to get off this damned thing onto a regular road where he might find a place to stay. He kept hoping that he'd drive out of this mess. He was heading west, and didn't the weather come from that direction? But the snowstorm seemed endless, and the terrain was unfamiliar. Back home they didn't get storms like this, but if they did, he knew the land almost as well as he knew himself and could practically drive blindfolded. But that was there, and while it was home, the walls had begun to shrink long ago, shaping themselves into proverbial bars and a door that he didn't want clanging shut behind him.

When he'd started out, this little adventure was supposed to be a lark, a chance to get away somewhere he could think for a while and maybe have the opportunity to be the man he was inside—the one he saw himself as.

But first he needed to get the hell out of this weather and off the freeway. Find some shelter and a warm place for the night. Then maybe he could have a chance to decide his next move.

He leaned forward to read a road sign through the blowing snow, then eased over to the exit that read Covington. Okay, it was at least a town. He took the snow-covered exit ramp and turned right onto a surprisingly clear road that led into the town, three miles away.

Three miles. It was starting to feel like a million.

George's hands ached from gripping the wheel, and he had to go something fierce. There was no one around, so he put on his four-ways and pulled off. The truck slid to a stop. George closed his coat around himself and opened the door. He instantly regretted it, but nature called and he had no choice.

He trudged around the other side of the truck, which acted as a windbreak, unzipped, and made fast work of the task at hand. Relief washed through him. At least that was one less worry. He zipped up and was hurrying around to the driver's side when movement across the road caught his eye—a dog, slinking along the gully. The skinny thing crossed the road and went down the other side before disappearing. He followed her quickly and found a dry culvert under the road. The dog lay at the entrance in a nest of sorts with four pups scurrying up to her.

"Jesus H. Christ," he muttered.

The mother dog, a reddish-brown bulldog mix, looked up at him with plaintive eyes.

George approached cautiously, looking around their home. There didn't seem to be any food, and the mother was emaciated as her pups clamored around her, mewling. She was starving herself for the sake of her pups, and none of them were going to make it very long in this weather. They were out of the wind, but the temperature was dropping. "You're a good mother, aren't you?" he whispered. She perked up and whined, desperation shining in her eyes.

There was no way he could leave them there, so he returned to the truck and dug around in back. He found an Amazon shipment box that had been there when he bought the truck. He brushed off the snow and folded open the sides before placing it on the floor. He lined it with the emergency blanket from the kit under the seat and reached behind to pull out the cooler. Then he closed the door and returned to where the mother stood.

George approached slowly and held out his hand, and she came right up to him and leaned against his leg as he stroked her.

"You're a sweetheart, aren't you?" he crooned and took a chance, lifting her up. She struggled, but George supported her butt and carried her to the truck, where he placed her in the box on the floor. Then he returned, scooped the squirming pups into his coat, and made a final check that he had the entire little doggie family before placing the pups in the box with her. They settled right in, and George raced to the driver's side and slid into the seat. He closed the door, started the engine, and cranked the heat.

Once it was warm, he opened the cooler. He had a few bottles of water, a couple of sandwiches, some soda, and a small bottle of milk, with an empty plastic potato salad container that he'd tossed in there a few hours ago. Knowing beggars couldn't be choosers, he used the salad container as a water dish and held it out to the mother, who drank like she was parched. Then he opened the wrapped roast beef sandwich and began feeding her pieces. At home he would never have thought of feeding the dogs human food. His father would have lectured him on the proper rearing of dogs... again. Everything had to be just so with his father and always the way he wanted it, with no discussion. That was part of the reason George was out here in the middle of nowhere. The chance at some freedom away from the heavy weight of responsibility for a while. The idea had been too good to pass up, but it had landed him in the middle of nowhere with a dog and her pups in an old truck he'd bought to make his trail harder to trace.

"You're all on your own, aren't you?" he asked quietly as he fed the dog. She had to be starving, but she was still gentle, and George wondered who could have thrown away a sweetheart like this with her pups. "Bloody bastards," he mumbled and fed her some more of the sandwich and let her drink the milk. He also gave a little to the pups to help supplement what she was feeding them. Having eaten, the puppies all quieted down, and George fed their mother the rest of the sandwich before she too settled down. George put the truck into gear and eased back onto the road.

It took ten minutes before the lights of the town came into view, and then he was in the middle of it. The main street was about two blocks long, and half the stores were dark, but at least they didn't look empty. It would have been terrible if he had wandered into a ghost town. He pulled up in front of a small store and left the engine running as he sat without moving, the tension of hours of driving in the blizzard finally catching up with him. He turned off the engine, got out and closed the door, pulled his coat closed, and hurried inside.

"We're just about to close," a kid said from behind the counter.

"Oh, sorry," he answered and rushed through the aisles with a trolley. He grabbed a bag of dog food and some puppy food, as well as a few toys. He got some food for himself and brought it up to the register, fishing dollars out of his wallet. "Is there a place to stay? A hotel or something?"

"The motel outside of town closed last year," the kid of maybe eighteen said. "That was it. There are a few people who rent rooms." He looked at the purchases. "But none of them allow dogs. What kind do you have?"

George sighed. "The kind with four puppies I found in a culvert half an hour ago. They were nearly frozen. I have them in my truck. I need a place where we can be warm until the snow ends." Warmth and a place to rest. That was all he needed. Oh, and to not have to drive anymore. That would be spectacular.

A phone rang, and the kid snatched it from under the counter. "Hi, Mom. ... Yeah, we're just closing up. Mr. Meyer told me to go home, and I'm about done." He looked at George. "I got one last customer. A man with an accent looking for a place to stay." He sounded like he was settling in for a talk. "Yeah, I told him, but he's got dogs...." He listened, and George looked out the windows to where the snow was already covering the truck windows. If he needed to find a place to stay, he'd best get out of here and back on the road. "Okay. Are you sure?" The kid looked George over a little dubiously. "Okay. Sure, Mom, if you think so. I'll call when I leave the store." He ended the call and finished ringing up the sale.

"Thanks." George hefted the bag into his arms. He wasn't particularly looking forward to getting back out on the road or to possibly sleeping in the truck if he couldn't find a place to stay, but this town didn't seem to have any prospects.

"My mother said that if you wanted to wait while I close up here, you can follow me. She says you can stay in the extra room off the kitchen for the night." He seemed more than a little suspicious. "She'll give you breakfast in the morning and you can be on your way. Mrs. Kline charges a hundred a night for her bed and breakfast place, so is that okay?"

George nodded even as he catalogued the cash he had on hand. It was more than enough. He wasn't using his charge cards so he could stay off the grid, but he had plenty. A place to stay would also mean that the dog and her pups could be warm, and he would have a chance to get them well fed before he tried to find them a home. "Thank you. I'll feed the dogs while I'm waiting." He was starting to worry about them getting cold in the truck. "I'm George Lester." Okay, so he fibbed a little on the last name, but he didn't want to take any chances.

"Fabian Justice." They shook hands, and George didn't remark on the unusual name. His mother must have been a fan of fifties music. "I know. People call me Chip." George wondered which was worse, but he didn't say anything. It wasn't his business what anyone called the kid, and all he wanted was to get out of the cold. He'd spend the night and then move on toward San Francisco in the morning. There, he figured he could blend into the city and have the time of his life for a little while.

"Thank you. And it's okay to bring the dogs?" George asked.

"Sure." Chip started closing up, and George returned to the truck and started the engine to warm things up. He also gave mama pupper some more food and water. Once he got a chance, he'd give the pups some milk-softened puppy food to supplement what Mama was giving them. He had seen that done back home to help take some strain off the mother.

Most of the lights in the store went off, and Chip came out, locked up, and headed to a truck parked a little ways down the road. George finessed the truck into gear and backed out, then followed the red work vehicle out of town and down whited-out country roads that left him wondering if he was being led to a scene out of *Deliverance*.

The pups whined a little, and the mother looked up at him with tired eyes. "I'm doing my best, girl. Keep your pups settled and we'll be there soon." *I hope*, he added to himself, afraid to speed up and hoping he didn't lose the red taillights ahead of him. He'd never had to navigate a storm like this at home. Winters were milder. They got snow, but never a real whopper like this.

Ahead, Chip slowed and turned into a driveway, and George followed him to a makeshift car park near the house. The dogs seemed to spring into action, woofing softly as soon as he pulled to a stop. George sighed and settled them once again before getting out, the wind nearly tumbling him over.

"Get your stuff and hurry inside," the young man called as snow whipped around him.

"What about the dogs?" he asked, and Chip hurried over.

"Let's bring them into the house. There's a mudroom where they'll be warm, and it won't matter when the pups pee." Chip opened the door and looked inside. "What a pretty girl. You've had it hard, haven't you, Mama?" George was right behind him. He lifted the mama into his arms while Chip got the pups. He could come back for his things once the dogs were settled and warm.

Chip led him to the back door, which opened, and he charged inside with George right behind. The warmth hit him like a wall, and he inhaled deeply just to get the cold out of his lungs.

"Well, look at that," a woman George assumed was Chip's mother said as she bustled in with an old blanket that she placed in the corner. "She's a tired girl." The mama dog—she was already Daisy in George's mind—settled on the blanket, and the pups snuggled in as soon as Chip set them down. Then Chip's mother put up an old baby gate, and they looked right at home. "Well, that's quite a little family." She turned to George, and he got his first real look at her. Black hair streaked with a little gray, warm eyes, and ruddy skin that had seen more than its fair share of sun and wind.

"Thank you, ma'am," George said, remembering the manners that had been drilled into him since he was old enough to walk. "Manners matter," his nanny had told him over and over. Though somehow George figured her lessons on when to use a fish fork weren't going to be needed out here.

"Call me Maureen. And no one should be caught out in this kind of storm," she said levelly, her demeanor more businesslike than it had been with the dogs. "Chip said you were looking for a place to stay for the night." He nodded. "Then go get your bags, and when you come back in, I'll show you to the room."

George thanked her again and hurried out to grab his suitcase from behind the seat. He also took the cooler and muscled the bag of things from the store, using his foot to kick the truck door closed. Then he scurried toward the back door, hoping the wind didn't unbalance him enough to send him ass-over-teakettle into the snow.

He made it inside, and Chip took the bags of dog food and set them on a shelf. George then set the cooler aside and took off his coat, which he folded over his arm.

The door opened, and a man covered with snow came inside, slamming the door against the wind. "Who's this?" he demanded. He pulled off his cowboy hat and gloves, and sparklingly cold blue eyes took George in with laser intensity.

"His name is George, and he's going to stay here tonight," Chip said, not intimidated by the wide-shouldered man. "Look at the dog and pups. He rescued them from the side of the road." Chip added the last part as though it somehow qualified him to stay. George didn't understand the dynamic.

"Let me show you to your room while my oldest, Alan, gets out of his snowy things and remembers his manners." The snap in Maureen's tone reminded George of Nanny and her way of reprimanding without raising her voice. "Come, George," she said in that businesslike tone, and he followed her through an exceptionally tidy home and through the kitchen to a closed door. She opened it and led him down a short hallway into the large sitting and sleeping area. "This was where my mother-in-law lived until she passed six months ago. I turned up the heat in here when Chip said he was bringing someone home."

"Thank you for this," George said softly. "I know having a stranger in your house probably isn't what you were expecting on a night like this, but I really do appreciate it." He took the money from his wallet and handed it to her. "This is what Chip and I agreed to. I hope it's still okay?"

"If Chip agreed," she said, taking the money in a slightly shaky hand. "Dinner will be in half an hour, and the bathroom is right in there." She turned and left him alone, closing the door behind her.

There was still a chill in the room, but it was definitely warmer than outside. George checked that he was moderately presentable, washed his face and hands, and then left the room and wandered toward the kitchen, which was filled with the scents of beef, roast potatoes, and other things he couldn't immediately place. He hadn't intended to overhear anything, but couldn't help catching Alan's voice.

"Why would you just take in a stranger?"

"Weren't you just outside?" Chip responded. "And it was Mom's idea," he added in that little-brother tone, which had George chuckling to himself. No more was said, and George sat at the table to be out of the way. Chip bustled in, with his mother close behind. She got to checking things in the kitchen, and Chip examined the dogs. It was pretty special, the way he talked to all of them as he looked the five dogs over. "That's a good girl. I'm not going to hurt your babies." George smiled as Chip checked over each pup and gave the mother a little more food. Then he left them alone, and the group seemed to settle.

"Don't worry about the pups," Maureen said, seemingly following his gaze. "Animals love Chip. We have a bull who hates everyone. Whenever Alan tries to come near him, he charges, but danged if he doesn't follow Chip like a puppy. Likes to get his butt scratched. If anyone else tried, he'd gore them." She peered into the oven and stood back up, keeping busy. "He's going to be a vet."

"And Alan?" George asked, assuming he was the gruff and suspicious one from earlier.

She smiled, clearly a proud parent no matter what she might say. "That one's a cowboy through and through. Rides in the local rodeo and manages the herd here on the ranch." The wind whipped outside the house, but she didn't seem to notice it, even though George could feel it, the change in air pressure pressing at his temples.

Speak of the devil, Alan strode in, boots gone, red socks on his feet. He sat across from George, hair disheveled, skin red, probably from the shower. "What were you doing out in that?" he asked.

"Heading west," George answered. "The snow started, and I thought I could drive out of it. No such luck. Then I found Daisy out there with her pups, and I couldn't let them freeze, so I brought them into the truck and stopped in the store, where I met Chip." He flashed the younger man a smile, but his gaze went right back to Alan's—broody blue eyes that seemed to see right down deep into him. Maybe it was the whole cowboy mystique thing. Alan certainly looked like the whole cowboy package. Hair a little rough, the line where he wore his hat still visible. Lines around his mouth and eyes, probably from so much time outdoors. Rough hands that George couldn't help wondering what they'd feel like against his skin.

Alan stood once again and opened one of the cupboards, treating George to the sight of a tight ass of stone encased in a pair of low-slung jeans. Narrow hips, wide shoulders, a body built from hard work. George couldn't help glancing at himself. Sure, he'd worked, but not like Alan or Chip. His work was totally different and so not suited for him. Or at least he'd never seemed to find his place there. Everyone needed to fit in somewhere, and George never had.

"What do you raise on your farm?" George asked.

"Cattle, so it's a ranch," Alan corrected. George nodded, getting the idea that he'd somehow insulted him. "Where are you from? The accent is…."

"England. Northumberland to be exact," George answered truthfully, though he didn't want to give them any more information than that. "Beautiful country. This area could be a lot like home, when it isn't covered by feet of snow. It's rugged there."

"Why are you here, then?" Alan asked. "What are you hoping for?" He put glasses on the table and sat back down.

"A chance to see some of the world." He gave his practiced answer. That was probably the best idea.

"That's enough, Alan. He's entitled to his business. You get the table ready for dinner, and then you'll have to check the barn before bed tonight." Maureen didn't brook any argument, and Alan helped carry things to the table. Chip washed up and did the same. Still, George noticed that Alan kept on eye on him, like he wasn't sure about him. Which was fine, because George definitely wasn't so sure about Alan either, or what it was he saw when Alan looked at him so intently.

CHAPTER 2

THERE WAS something off about the man Chip had brought home for the night. Alan couldn't put his finger on it, but leave it to his little brother to bring home a stray… and one with a set of strays of his own. Not that it mattered. The guy would be gone in the morning and their lives would return to normal. Alan had plenty to do anyway, and it wasn't like the uppity-sounding guy was going to stick around. He was too prim and proper for this area.

Alan didn't doubt that the guy was just passing through. Life out here in ranch country was hard, and this guy didn't look like he'd done a full day's work in his life. Not that it was any of Alan's business, though he couldn't help looking, and looking didn't hurt anyone. The man was something to see, after all. Almost flaming red hair and eyes that seemed to take in everything. And if the story about the dogs was true, then the guy couldn't be all bad. Chip seemed to like him well enough, and Alan had to admit that his little brother had pretty good people instincts. After all, he'd warned Alan about Eustice. Alan had hired him last summer to help on the ranch, and he'd caught him asleep on the job twice and then trying to get into the house when he had no business there. Alan had fired him, and Chip had given him the "I told you so" look that Alan hated, especially from his little brother.

"What do you do back in Northumberland?" Alan asked between bites of his mom's roast beef. She could cook just about anything and make it taste like a feast, that was for sure.

"I work in the family business. I'm what you might call an executive." He seemed to choose his words carefully, or maybe it was just the accent, but Alan knew this guy was hiding something, if only by the way he lowered his gaze whenever he answered a question.

"So you sit in an office all day? Sounds terrible."

"Not everyone likes to work out in the sun, wind, heat, and cold all the time," Chip said, rolling his eyes. "Not everyone is you."

Alan humphed and finished his dinner. He took his plate to the sink and then, with a final look, pulled on boots and his outdoor gear before escaping the kitchen. He needed to get the heck out of there. The room was becoming too warm, and he had work to do. That gave him an excuse to get out of the house and away from George.

Once he was dressed for the cold, he hurried outside, following the light on the barn through the blowing snow. He pulled the door closed behind him.

The cattle had plenty of feed, and he had already made sure they were bedded down in a sheltered spot for the night. He checked on each of the horses and found Maribelle looking at him, straining.

"Damn." He hadn't been expecting the chestnut mare to give birth this soon, and it looked like she was in trouble. Alan calmed her and felt her belly and sides for the foal, trying to see which way it was turned. It had felt right to him when he last checked. She seemed ready to give birth, but the foal wasn't coming.

Shit—he had seen this before. With her last foal, Maribelle had struggled, and then the foal had come almost as if someone had flipped a switch. But this was worse, and she was really hurting.

Alan patted her neck and did his best to calm her. "I'm going to help you, girl." He stepped away and sent a message to Chip at the house. He was going to need his help too. Alan hoped he wasn't going to have to pull the foal. That could mean that they'd lose the mother or the foal, and sometimes both. Alan didn't want any of those scenarios to happen. He needed Maribelle. She was an amazing horse, and he was counting on selling the foal so they could make up some of last year's shortfall. The ranch was just hanging on, and they all needed a break if they were going to have a chance to get ahead.

I'm on my way, Chip answered, and Alan continued calming the horse, even as she whinnied harder, her sides contracting as her body tried to give birth, but things just weren't cooperating. He waited for Chip and was surprised when George came out as well. He went right around, looking at her intently.

"She's in distress," George said calmly.

"I know," Alan commented shortly. He hated that the stress was getting to him. "The foal has turned."

"Hold her still."

"You need to get away," Alan said as a warning.

George ignored him and wet his hands from the hose, speaking quietly to Maribelle. His voice alone seemed to calm her before George checked up inside Maribelle. She started, and Chip held Maribelle while Alan tried to calm her. "The foal is right there…." George gasped. "But I think his hoof is…." He withdrew his hand and backed away as the front hooves made an appearance, followed by the head and then the rest of the body. The birth flowed much more easily from there and the little horse was born in less than a minute. "Just a small adjustment."

"You're a fool to do that with a horse that doesn't know you," Alan chastised and then calmed slightly. "How did you know what to do?" Alan asked. "I would normally call the vet, but in this weather he wouldn't be able to get here." He got out of the stall as Maribelle went into mother mode, encouraging the little colt to stand. He got up on wobbly legs and started to nurse. Chip brought George a rag and a towel so he could wash up, the man smiling warmly. Okay, maybe he'd been hasty to judge.

"My family has horses, and I trained to work with animals," George answered, but once again Alan got the sense that there was something George wasn't saying. Still, he obviously knew his stuff and had saved the day. "We need to make sure the stall is cleaned right away and that she has plenty of hay and some extra oats. The birth was hard on her, and she'll need her energy."

Alan knew that, but he didn't say the snipe that came to mind. He owed George a debt of gratitude. They could have lost both the mother and the colt.

"He's gorgeous, Alan," Chip said in that way he had when talking about animals. They had always been first in his little brother's heart ever since he was five years old and befriended a barn cat that had injured his paw. Chip had rescued the feral thing, and damned if that frickin' cat hadn't trusted Chip right away. Some of his children and grandchildren still kept the barn free of vermin. "Look at the coloring—the white star on his forehead."

"Yeah. The black is beautiful. Was the sire that color?" George asked, looking over at Alan.

Alan shrugged. "We weren't sure who the sire was. I hadn't planned on breeding her, but she seemed to have her own ideas and got out. It seems she bred with one of the neighbor's stallions before we found her about eight hours later." He winked. "She's one randy girl. I have a pretty good idea which stallion it was now, and Connor is going to be pissed."

George gave him a curious look. "Why?"

"The father is Rampart. He's Connor's major draw, and every one of his colts sells for a great deal. And this little guy is going to be in that category. Look at his conformation and coloring. They're going to line up for him. All we have to do is prove that Rampart is the father, and a genetic test should do the trick." Chip smiled.

"But we have to get a sample for testing, and Connor will never give us one."

"Actually, you don't. Do you know of a verified Rampart foal? Have him tested against that foal. That should tell if they have the same sire. No Connors involved." George leaned against the stall door, and Alan saw that smile. It seemed genuine, like he let himself go for just a moment. Then the mask slipped into place once again.

Every man had a right to his own thoughts and his privacy. Alan was still concerned but willing to let George be... for now. He was staying in the house with his mother and little brother, and Alan took his role as the man and protector of the family very seriously. Three years ago, his father on his deathbed, Alan had sat with him, and his father had made him promise that he would take care of his mother and see to it that Chip got the education he needed. He also made him promise to step up and take care of the family, and that was what he'd done. His mother ran the house the way she always did, and Alan had stepped into his father's large boots and done his best to fill them. A year out of high school, when other guys his age were away at school or raising hell, he was running the ranch and making sure his family was taken care of. It was his job, and Alan intended to see it through. It didn't matter if a sexy, mysterious stranger took refuge at the house during a storm... and managed to save Maribelle and her colt. He wasn't going to let his guard down for anyone or any reason.

Chip made sure there were oats and hay aplenty for Maribelle, along with ample water. The colt was nursing well and staying close to her. "We'll move them to a fresh stall in the morning. I don't want to do it right now, but I want them in one with fresh hay."

They all took a last look at the new colt, and then Alan ushered them out of the barn. He'd check on the colt later before he went to bed, but for now, mama and son needed some time alone without an audience. Alan left some of the lights on and closed the barn door against the wind, then hurried them all over to the house and inside.

"Maribelle's colt is doing well. George rescued him and Maribelle. It was awesome." Chip was all energy, and Mom seemed relieved. She knew the stakes. "The sire seems to be Rampart," Chip went on. "That should make him pretty valuable once we prove it."

"Okay," she said indulgently. "I made some apple pie, so cut slices for everyone." She sat in her chair the way she always did in the evenings when the work was done, her knitting needles going a mile a minute. Alan sat as well, closing his eyes, the soft clicks soothing his ragged nerves. George stayed on the periphery for a few seconds and then excused himself, and a moment later the door to the back room closed quietly.

"He seems nice enough," Alan said.

His mom nodded without pausing in her work. She seemed to be making a hat of some sort, which was good, because they always needed winter gear. "He'll be gone tomorrow," she said softly. "So then maybe you can let go of your bulldog attitude and just relax for an hour or so."

He leaned forward. "How am I supposed to do that with him in the house?"

She sighed. "Son, did Chip exaggerate?" Alan shook his head. "Then that man just saved the ranch's entire profit for the next six months, in addition to Maribelle. He did you and all of us a favor. Not only that, but he paid for the night already, and that's the next week's trip to the grocery store with what we have put up." His mother had a way of looking at the practical.

But it was Alan's job to watch for threats. "And what about all those dogs?"

"Do you really think your brother is going to let that mama and her litter of pups go tomorrow? He'll offer to take them and raise them because that's who your brother is." She rolled her eyes.

Chip brought in some slices of pie and handed him one and one to his mother. Then he took the extra plate he had into the other room.

"Think of it this way. Maybe George was supposed to come here. Maybe that was the bigger plan… just so he could save Maribelle and the colt." She put her knitting aside and ate her slice of pie. "My mother used to say that everything happens for a reason."

Now it was Alan's turn for an eye roll. "And Grandma used to wear her bra on the outside of her blouse part of the time, so I don't know if I'm buying that as an argument or not." His mother smiled and then laughed. She didn't do that enough. In fact, Alan figured none of them did. They spent so much time working and trying to get through each day in one piece that there wasn't a lot of time or energy left over for that sort of thing.

"Where's George?" his mother asked Chip when he returned.

"In his room. I took him some pie, and he stayed in there. I think he's tired. I told him that I would see that Daisy and her puppies were all right for the night. I also need to take her outside before bed and put down papers and stuff for the pups." He plopped down on the sofa on the opposite side from his mom. "I checked the weather, and the report says that the storm will run all night and isn't supposed to let up until late tomorrow. So we're not going anywhere for at least two days." He took a bite of pie with a grin.

"Great," Alan muttered.

"We have plenty of provisions for us and the herd. Since he can't leave, maybe he'll help you get out and check that the herd has enough food."

Alan groaned deep in his throat.

Chip ignored it, as usual. "He's a good guy, and he helped Maribelle. And he didn't shy away from doing the unpleasant stuff. So back off, Alan. Jeez. The guy rescued puppies in a blizzard, and he saved Maribelle and little Centauri." Chip jumped to his feet, glaring hard at Alan like he was the bad guy here.

Alan's head started to hurt. Couldn't they understand that they had no idea who this George was? He was a guy Chip picked up at work and brought home because he needed a place to stay. The fact that he sent all of Alan's Spidey senses through the roof was only another reason for him to watch. "What if…." Alan tried to be reasonable, but he ended up growling and stood, looking over Chip. "Wait, Centauri? You don't get to name the colt."

"And you do?" Chip challenged. "I'll call him Centauri, and you can come up with any dumb name you want. He has a star on his forehead, and Alpha Centauri is the closest star system to our sun, so I thought that would be a great name for him." He put his hands on his hips, foot forward.

"That's enough testosteronal posturing. Alan, sit down. I like the name, but Chip, Alan is right. You have to talk it over with all of us." Mom continued her knitting, and Alan sat back down, glaring at his little brother, who did the same.

"Fine." Alan humphed. "You can call the colt what you want. But I'm still reserving judgment." He finished his pie and then brought his plate to the kitchen and set it in the sink. He nearly bumped into George as he came out. Alan hadn't realized he'd left his room, and he wondered if George had heard him and Chip talking.

"I'm sorry. I know this is awkward," George said gently, his eyes soft, even as he stood tall and rather stiffly, almost like he was in the military or something. "I will be gone just as soon as I possibly can." His accent grew heavier and his gaze sharp. "I don't want to cause any trouble for any of you." He held his head up and passed Alan in the hall before turning at the end of it.

Alan told himself that he wasn't going to watch him go, but he did it anyway. There was something in the way George wrapped himself in dignity and propriety that both irked and fascinated him.

George looked at him just before stepping out of sight, and Alan hurried into the bathroom and closed the door. Fucking hell, not only had he been caught looking, but in that split second, George seemed to see right through him, like he'd just stripped Alan bare. He shook his head to dispel the ridiculous notion. He cleaned up and took care of business before leaving the room.

"I appreciate all this very much," George was saying in the living room. "And I know this is an imposition."

"Storms like this happen a couple times a year," his mother said gently. "Hospitality and kindness to strangers are something that everyone takes pretty seriously out here. We all survive with the help of our neighbors and the community." Alan quietly went down the hall to where George stood in front of his mother. George gave her a small bow and then took her hand.

"You are a princess among people," he said softly before gently kissing her fingers. Then he straightened up and practically swept out of the room.

Alan shook his head as he went to the mudroom and closed the door, looking at the mama dog and her beautiful pups. He wondered about the strange gesture and the way George kissed his mother's hand. What Alan needed to do was check on Maribelle and Centauri before going to bed so he could get up early and get some work done, regardless of the weather. The cattle needed to be tended, and he had to ensure that they survived this storm or else there would be nothing left of the ranch.

Alan pulled on his winter gear and charged out into the wind and snow, heading for the barn, where he found mother and colt snug in their stall, the colt pressed to his mother. The inside of the barn was warm, but Alan slipped a light blanket over Maribelle to help her retain heat and made sure all the mangers had hay and the stalls had fresh water. On a night like this, they all needed some extra fuel.

Alan took a few minutes with the horses, letting them calm the roiling inside him. After a while, he figured everyone would be in bed, so he left the barn, closed the door tight, and returned to the house, hoping that the worst of the winds were past them. Inside, he hung his coat in the mudroom, where Daisy was curled up in her bed with the puppies asleep. She thumped her tail a few times and then settled down. Alan gave her a gentle pat before heading through the quiet house to his own bedroom.

He stripped down and climbed under the covers, intent on going right to sleep, but his mind kept conjuring George's image. The thing was, Alan knew he should be vigilant since there was a stranger in the house, and that he should protect the family. But his libido seemed more interested in the way George looked at him, and that flaming red hair, and eyes that seemed to light a fire inside Alan that he wished he could figure out how to douse. Not that it mattered. Alan wasn't going to act on anything, and George would be gone just as soon as the storm let up, and it would be the end. It was that simple.

So why in the hell couldn't he get George out of his increasingly vivid imagination?

Chapter 3

A KNOCK ON the door had George bolting upright in bed. It took him a minute to remember where he was, with the near pitch blackness that surrounded him. Yeah, he was in Wyoming, and from the whistling outside, the wind was still blowing.

The knock came again, and George got out of bed, shivering until he pulled on his pants and answered the door. Light crept in from the other room. "Is something wrong? Is it the colt or Daisy?" he asked, blinking into Alan's eyes.

Alan was already dressed—or mostly dressed, his shirt barely buttoned, giving George a nice partial view of a chest dusted with dark hair—and carried a mug of coffee. "Nothing like that. Chip is out in the barn with them and has been for much of the night."

George swallowed around the lump in his throat, because… damn. If this was what real cowboys looked like, then he was more than ready to ride the range. "Okay." He was a little confused. "What time is it?"

"Nearly six," Alan answered.

He groaned. "So why did you get me up?" That was way too early to be awake on a day like this. He'd rather sleep and just be warm for a while.

"I need your help," Alan answered. "The weather has made things more difficult for us. It's still snowing, and it's already deep. I have a good idea where the herd is, but I need some help getting feed out to them. They'll take shelter from the wind, but without food, they'll freeze." He seemed worried.

George had grown up in the country, and he knew just how much folks relied on their animals to survive. They gave eggs, meat, milk, even skins and hair, all of which country folk—ranchers or farmers—depended on to survive. "You want me to go out in that?" he asked. George had never been out in a blizzard like that, but he had brought animals in during gales where the rain came at him from the side. And he knew that sometimes things just needed to be done.

Alan drew closer, his rich, slightly musky but fresh scent tickling George's nose, and George inhaled deeply just to take it in. "Look, I can't do this alone, and Chip is taking care of the barn. Normally I'd have a neighbor go out with me, but we're in a bit of a fix with the weather. No one is going anywhere, and we're all stuck where we are. The roads are drifted shut, so...."

"Okay. Let me put on some warm clothes. I don't have any wellies with me. Maybe I can borrow some?" He turned on one of the lights beside the bed and hunted in his bags. He figured layers would be best and started setting out clothes.

"What are those?" Alan asked.

"Wellies? Sorry. Boots," he answered, translating to American. "I have shoes, but not boots." He probably should have bought a pair, but he had expected to be in San Francisco by now.

"Between Chip and myself, we should have something for you," Alan replied. "Get dressed and come to the kitchen. Mom is making something to eat, and then we'll head out." He turned, and George took in the spectacular view as he rolled his eyes. He wondered if Alan was naturally gruff or if he worked at it. Still, George was here and not going anywhere, so he might as well help out.

George found it interesting that here, when the work needed to be done, he was asked to help, but it was almost assumed that he'd chip in. The request had none of the deference that it would have been cloaked in at home. Someone would have explained the problem, and then everyone would have looked at him expectantly, like he was supposed to decide the next steps to solve it. He liked this way better. These people knew their business, even if their lives were hard work. George pulled on a pair of light sweatpants and then a pair of jeans over them. Then he got out two pairs of socks and rolled them on before slipping a T-shirt over his head, then a button-down, followed by a sweatshirt. He knew that the best way to combat the cold was layers. He had his coat and a hat, as well as leather gloves, so he figured he was ready.

A plate had already been set at the table, and Maureen put a stack of pancakes on it. Alan was wolfing down his breakfast, but George took his time, adding some syrup and tasting the pancakes. His appetite kicked in quickly, and he began eating faster, wondering if this was like eating with the queen and he had better be done when Alan was. Those meals were always an "eat before you get there" affair, just in case.

"I have some boots that might fit you and some heavy work gloves. They're in the mudroom." Maureen bustled around the kitchen. "I fed and took Daisy out to do her business, as well as cleaned up after the puppies. She's doing a lot better." She smiled his way. "You got there in time. It's doubtful they would have survived out there in this weather."

"She's a sweet girl," George said, continuing to eat ravenously, but still with manners. Years of training were hard to ignore. Once the food was gone, he took his plate to the sink the way he'd seen the others do and thanked Maureen before getting the boots, which were a little too big. He grabbed another pair of socks and put them on, and then the boots fit better. The gloves were much better suited than the ones he had, and by the time he was ready, Alan was shrugging into his coat and pulling a hat onto his head.

"We need to get going." He charged out the door like he was a knight going into battle, and maybe that's what Alan thought he had to do. George did his best to keep up and joined Alan at one of the sheds, where the wind had piled snow up to his neck against the doors. Alan handed him a shovel, and George began digging next to him. At least the snow was loose and they were able to clear it. Then Alan opened the wide doors to reveal two large snowmobiles. "Have you driven one of these before?"

"No."

"Then you're in for a treat," Alan said. He showed George how to control one. Then he started the engine and pulled the machine out. "Go down the drive and back just to get the feel for it. I'll lead so you can follow in my tracks." He turned to get the other one, and George climbed on the thrumming machine and took it forward a little. It hummed under him, and he smiled before going faster. It was like gliding over the snow, and he loved it. He made a turn and resisted the urge to lean into it too much, keeping his weight as close to center as he could. Once he returned, Alan motioned him over, and they began loading bales of feed onto the back racks and tying them down with elastic cords.

"Is this how you usually do it?" George asked.

"No. But we do what we have to. I'll go first, and just take it easy. Once we reach the herd, we can get the bales to them. We may need to make a couple of trips," Alan said over the wind and then climbed on his snowmobile and started forward. George did as he was instructed, pulling on the helmet and goggles Alan had given him.

George felt a little like an abominable snowman in all this gear, but he was glad he had it as they started out over the snow. The wind buffeted him from the west, and he had to steer to keep it from pushing him off course. Alan pointed ahead and off to the left, so George went in that direction, opening up the throttle a little more. He loved speed, and this was like snow flying.

Black dots appeared up ahead once they crested a small rise. The cattle were clustered together near a rock outcropping that seemed largely free of snow. Alan slowed, and he and George approached cautiously, probably so they didn't startle any of the animals. They rode pretty close, and then Alan pulled to a stop, took a bale off the back, pulled off the string, and tossed it away, maybe ten feet. The hay bale split apart, and the cattle headed over. Damn, he was strong. The bales were heavy, and yet Alan handled them like they weighed next to nothing. He did the same with the second and third bales, while George unhooked his.

"Put yours over there. That way they all won't try to eat from the same area," Alan said.

George complied, watching the cattle as they trudged over and started to eat. "They're stunning animals," George said, watching the steers. "And well taken care of."

"You know cattle?" Alan asked.

George nodded. "I've worked with them." Actually, with the price of beef in England, he had started building a herd of his own on part of his family's land in order to diversify their holdings. He watched as they made their way through the lighter covering of snow to the food. "We're going to need at least another run. They can't reach the grass, and I bet what there is isn't going to be much help to them now."

"You're right," Alan said, looking at him quizzically. "When I first saw you, I never would have pegged you as someone who knew about cattle."

"Or was willing to stick his hands up the business end of a horse?" George asked, liking this part of Alan—the non-smartass part. He cocked an eyebrow. "Where I come from, everyone helps out when necessary. Even me."

He wished he'd left the last part of that statement off. It was true, but back home, people tended to be a little surprised when he showed up to help with the cows or the sheep. George had no idea why. It was something he'd always done, and yet it always took folks by surprise. Maybe that was because his father would never have done that sort of thing. It had been beneath his dignity. And maybe that was part of why they hadn't gotten along, though George now wished they had. "Now, should we go back for another load? This wind isn't going to let up, and the snow isn't stopping."

"Chip checked the weather, and the forecast said the wind would let up. I sure hope it does that soon and this passes by."

"Is this normal?" George asked. Storms at home came in and moved on. This one seemed to be lingering.

"It happens, but usually not quite this bad." Alan jumped on the snowmobile and took off. George took off after him, opening up the machine and zooming over the snow. He loved the speed and the sensation of flying over the cover of white. Alan approached next to him, and George lowered his body and added more speed. This was turning into a race, and George's competitive streak kicked in. He hated to lose, but he didn't have the experience on these machines. Still, he pushed it, and he burst into the yard just ahead of Alan.

"I'll get you next time," Alan teased as they pulled to a stop next to the barn. "I thought you never rode one of these before."

"I haven't." But he had driven some really fast cars and loved the speed and the thrill of besting the next driver. "Beginner's luck?" he offered so he didn't offend Alan, who actually smiled. Damn, that was a sight.

"We'll see," he retorted and began loading the hay on the cargo racks for the next trip out to the herd. George helped, and soon they were on the way back. George was wearing half his wardrobe and working hard, but the cold was relentless. They reached the herd, and George added the bales to their feeding areas, the cattle content and seemingly not bothered by the cold weather.

"What about water?" George asked.

"The creek is spring-fed, so it runs all year long." Alan pointed over to where a dark pool ran along the landscape. "They'll follow that trail down to the edge to drink." He finished up and then led the way over on the snowmobile. Cattle approached the edge, drank their fill, and threaded their way back through the snow toward the hay. It was like the cattle all knew the routine and kept it up regardless of the weather.

"We should get back," Alan said, looking up to where the sun would be if it had been visible. He pulled out his phone and tugged off a glove. "It looks like the snow will stop in the next few hours, and they're saying the wind will die as well."

"That's good, isn't it?" George asked.

"It depends on when the cloud cover dissipates. Hopefully it will last until morning. If it doesn't, it's going to get damned cold, and then no windbreak is going to help them." He turned back toward the herd, worrying his lower lip. Alan had seemed strong and impenetrable, yet that one gesture showed his worry. George liked it. It meant Alan was human after all. He also understood it, and how putting the herd in danger put everything he'd worked for in jeopardy.

"What does the forecast say?" George asked.

"One site is betting the clouds will hold, while another has it getting really cold by morning." He swallowed. "All we can do is make sure these beasts have enough feed to generate the internal heat to keep them warm. I've also seen them gather together to share warmth." He paused, and those huge eyes turned George's way. "There's nothing I can do about it at the moment. They're in a sheltered place, and there isn't enough barn space to bring them inside."

George nodded. "Another load, then?" he asked. Alan simply nodded, and they started back toward the ranch compound.

"Do you think they'll be all right?" Chip asked once they had finished their work and were back inside the house, the warmth of the kitchen finally taking away the chill that seemed to have reached all the way to Alan's bones.

"It's still windy and snowing. The storm seems to be letting up, but it isn't moving out too fast. I suspect, though, that tomorrow is going to be clear as a bell, which means the real challenge will be tomorrow night."

"We've weathered this before, and we will again," Maureen said gently. "This happens. It's part of our business."

George had to admire her fortitude, and that of Alan and Chip. They lived this every day, and he was just here until the weather changed before he moved on to warmer climes.

"Is there anything more I can do to help?" At least once he got warm again, because God.... He wrapped his hands around the coffee mug Maureen set in front of him, using it to warm his fingers.

"No," Chip answered. "This is just part of the worry. We go through this with the weather all the damned time. This past summer it was a tornado that swept through a mile away. Didn't touch us, but scared everyone. The Gundersons lost their barn in it, and we all went over to help them rebuild."

"Chip," Maureen said lightly.

"But it's true. We worry and talk about what might happen, but none of us can control the weather. It's the one thing we're at the mercy of." He pushed back his chair and left the table, probably for some puppy time with Daisy and the little ones. Not that George could blame him.

"Just go on in to rest. You did your part already," Alan told George. "I'd still be out there for another hour if you hadn't helped with the feed, and they should be fine." He met George's gaze, and suddenly the cold vanished. The respect and maybe even a touch of heat in those now deep blue eyes made George swallow. George wondered if Alan's family was aware of his sexuality.

George had been to boarding school and university in England, and he knew interest when he saw it. He was no blushing flower or huge closet case, but where he came from, things were often done the way they had been for decades, and attitudes tended to be slow to change. So while he never denied who he was to folks who might have asked, he wasn't out there beating drums at Pride gatherings either. Maybe that was part of why he was running away. George sipped his coffee, his gaze sliding to Alan, and wondered if the people around him understood who he really was.

Not that George had any doubt that Alan was a cowboy. The mystique settled on him like the snow falling outside. But it was tough maintaining a façade all the time. George should know, because his family motto was to always appear as though everything was perfect no matter what. His mother nearly died when he was sixteen, and yet his father still went to the local pub every Friday to keep up appearances that everything was fine, because that was what people expected of him. If he didn't go, there would be talk, and that was something his father would never have allowed. Talk meant weakness and cracks in the image of perfection that he cultivated for himself and the family. George was always expected to keep up that image, and being gay certainly didn't fit. His parents knew his "proclivities," as they put it, but they ignored them and expected him to act with proper discretion. Which basically meant that as long as he was quiet and lived his life out of the public eye, he was fine, but should anyone find out he was gay… well, that was a different matter entirely.

George went into the other room, and soon Daisy trotted in with the pups and Chip right behind her. He settled on the floor with the puppies crawling over him, and he laughed and gave gentle caresses while Daisy sat against his leg, watching intently. "She's probably wondering if you're going to leave them," Chip said.

George shook his head. "Nope."

Chip sat cross-legged on the floor, and the reddish puppies crawled over his legs to get a place on his lap.

"I had dogs at home. Mostly hunting dogs. My father didn't allow them in the house." He wasn't going to recount what he said about the dogs. It wasn't for polite company, and nothing good could come of it. George stroked Daisy's head. She was such a good dog. "Why would anyone just dump her and the puppies off?" he wondered out loud.

"Because some people are complete bastards," Alan commented dryly, and he sat in one of the chairs and propped his socked feet up on the scarred coffee table. It didn't take George long to figure out where those scars had come from, and he climbed into a chair, adding his feet to the table. Daisy kept watching him, and George looked at the others before patting his lap. Daisy bounded up and lay across his legs.

"You say that like you know who it might be." George watched as Chip and Alan exchanged glances. "I see." He got the picture pretty clearly.

"Connor, next door," Chip said as he gently petted the puppies until they all seemed to be falling asleep right there in a pile. "He found a cat last year, and I saw him trying to get rid of it on the road to the highway. I picked it up, and it's now in our barn. I suppose he'd do that with a dog and puppies if he wanted them gone."

"Like I said, a heartless bastard," Alan added in a low growl.

"That's enough of that talk," Maureen chided. She sat in the empty chair and picked up her knitting. "Hank Connor…," she began, and then let the thought die on her lips. "I don't want any more said about him."

Chip reached for the remote and turned on the television. "Thankfully the storm is letting up, so the satellite is back," he said with a smile and settled against the sofa to watch a rerun of *Special Victims Unit*. It turned into a quiet family moment, and George wondered if he should go to his room and leave them alone. It felt almost intrusive to be part of how comfortable they were with each other.

"I've got to go back out to check on everything in a few hours," Alan said quietly.

"I'll handle the barn and stuff," Chip said. "Centauri is a feisty one. I think he's really going to be something else." He sat until the end of the episode, then turned off the television and gently carried the pups back to the mudroom. Daisy followed, and they settled in once more while George dressed to go out with Alan. If these people were good enough to let him stay, then he was going to help. Those were the best kind of manners.

After he and Alan were done for the evening, he took off his gear in the mudroom and found Maureen in the living room. She turned to look at him and then fished through the television directory before clicking on a show. George knew exactly the one and cringed as his own face appeared on the screen. "So that is you," she said softly.

"Yes...," George answered. It was an episode of a Netflix show that an acquaintance had done back in Northumberland, about how his family made their ancestral estate pay in the twenty-first century.

She nodded at his answer and turned back to the screen. "I just have one question. What the hell is the Duke of Northumberland doing in Covington, Wyoming?" she asked just as Alan approached from behind him, and George felt his laser-like gaze on the back of his neck as any sort of goodwill he might have built with the stone-hard cowboy flew right out the window.

CHAPTER 4

"WHAT WERE you doing? Laughing at the country bumpkins as we opened our home to you?" Alan's eyes blazed. "Were you having a great big chuckle at us while we worked to try to save our living? Your Grace."

"That's enough, Alan," Mom said. "Give George a chance to explain."

Alan cleared his throat. "You can start with your fake name." He was angry and hurt. And to think that he'd actually started to like the guy. But it seemed he was just playing some kind of game.

"George is my name. Well, one of them. My full name is Albert Christopher Charles George Montague Lester, Eighth Duke of Northumberland." He stood tall and straight. "My parents named me after various family members in my father's as well as my mother's family. I rarely use all of them since it's a real mouthful. I chose George because it's the one I like the best. As for the rest, well, what meaning does a noble title have here?" Even at a time like this, there was a quiet dignity about him that Alan found... impressive, even as it got under his skin in a way few people could.

"Because it's part of who you are," Maureen added.

George shook his head. "That's where you're wrong. Back home in England, that's who I am. Here, I thought it was the way I acted, and that I would be judged and accepted based on what I did rather than the title I was born with." He held their gazes, and Alan found himself with a growing sense of embarrassment.

"But you lied to us."

George cleared his throat. "There were things about myself that I didn't tell you. But which of us doesn't have things they wish to keep to themselves? In Northumberland I'm the duke, the landowner who sits at the very top of the food chain. Everyone tells me what they think I want to hear and calls me either 'my lord' or 'your grace.' I had one lady the other day actually curtsy to me like I was the queen." The more he spoke, the more Alan noticed the light in George's eyes dim.

"Okay, fine. I get that, I guess...."

George turned to Alan. "When was I supposed to tell you? When I carried Daisy and her puppies into the mudroom, or when I had my hands up inside Maribelle to adjust the colt? Maybe I should have said something as I was hauling the hay and feed for the cattle." He shrugged.

"Were you ever going to say anything?" Maureen asked.

George shook his head. "No. I always thought that here a man would be accepted for his actions and nothing else. In the US, I'm George and nothing more. I was wrong to think that my title wouldn't follow me somehow. I had hoped it wouldn't be this quickly."

"So all that stuff you told me about things back home…?" Alan pushed on.

"Was true. I didn't make anything up. I told you what it was like back home. I have a herd of cattle on the estate to help diversify our holdings, and I have worked with plenty of horses. Some of them we race, and others we use for polo. My father was passionate about the game and used to play with one of the princes." He shrugged. "That isn't me. I went to university and then on to veterinary school. I finished and was going for the clinical portion of my training when my father died last year." George stiffened, and Alan thought he was going to go all formal, but then his shoulders slumped and he seemed defeated, like a burden that he didn't know how he was going to handle rested on his shoulders. "I expected the stubborn old goat to last forever, but he didn't." George swallowed, and Alan had this desire to try to comfort him, but he remained in place, reminding himself that George had lied to him and that the person he thought he might be starting to get to know wasn't real. He was just someone that the duke wanted them to know—he wasn't the real person underneath. At least that explained the reservations he'd had about him.

Chip burst in, his face alight. "Are you really a duke?" he asked, and Alan rolled his eyes. "Have you ever met the queen? Do you live in one of those huge houses like on *Downton Abbey*?"

George smirked a little. "Yes, I'm a duke—the title is inherited— and yes, I have met the queen on a few occasions. My great-grandfather knew her father, King George VI. And as for the house, yes, it's big, and it's like living in a museum. My mother opened the house to tourists, and now there are people touring it four or five months a year. And all of it is my responsibility and something I never wanted or was supposed to have to worry about." He bit his lower lip, and Alan knew there was more to the story.

"I think that's enough," Mom said. "Alan, a man is entitled to his privacy and to make his own decisions." She glared at him. "I raised you well enough to know that."

The rebuke stung. All he'd been doing was trying to protect his family.

"George will be with us for a few more days, judging by the weather report, which has just changed and has another storm approaching." She switched the station, and Alan groaned at the forecast of another eight to twelve inches of snow.

"We're going to need to get more feed out to the herd," Alan said.

"And the horses will need to be exercised. They've been in the barn for two days, and with another storm, they'll stay there longer," Chip added. "I was thinking we could clear one of the paddocks with the tractor and give the horses a chance to move. Do you think we can do that tomorrow before the next weather front comes in?"

Alan nodded, the list of things to do growing in his mind.

"I can help. I know horses and can ride. I can also help bring out feed like I did today," George offered.

Alan bit back the retort that formed on his lips about that being beneath His Grace.

"Thank you, George. That would be a big help," Mom said right away.

George nodded and left, the door to the room he was using closing quietly.

"What's wrong with you?" Chip snapped in a stage whisper.

"I wouldn't expect you to understand," Alan sniped back. "What the heck do we know about him other than what he told us?"

Chip pushed his iPad in front of him. "Lots. He has his own Wikipedia page, and it has a lot of stuff about him. He went to Eton, and the stuff about university and training as a vet is true." Chip looked some more and gasped. "He had an older brother who died four years ago. That's just sad." Chip then got the wicked little-brother look. "Though there are times…."

"Chip!" Mom scolded.

"He is a real pain in the ass sometimes," Chip defended.

"Language," she scolded. Alan noticed she didn't correct him on the substance of the comment.

Chip didn't look chastised for a second. "It makes sense. His older brother would inherit almost everything, so he was going to be a vet. His brother was killed in an accident, apparently while racing in a car, then his father died, and George is now the duke." He set the iPad on the coffee table. "I think I'd want to get out if that happened to me." He plopped down on the sofa. "And maybe I'd want people to look at me as a person rather than make assumptions because of a fancy title."

Alan scoffed. "Really? You wanted to be a country singer so you could be famous up until you realized you couldn't carry a tune in a bucket. And—"

Chip rolled his eyes again. "You know, I think you're so upset because you like the guy." He snickered and bounded off the sofa when Alan made a leap for him. "You got the hots for the duke?" He raced behind Mom's chair, cackling.

Alan hurried toward him, and Chip leapt again, this time toward the hall.

"Boys, that's enough. Chip, stop picking on your brother." She narrowed her gaze. "And since you're going to be exercising the horses, you can clean out the barn while they're in the paddock." Chip groaned, and Alan kept his satisfaction to himself. "And you...." She glared at Alan with that look he knew too damned well.

"I already have plenty to do," he grumped, and he left the room, got on his gear, and headed outside.

It was dark. He went to the barn, where he climbed into the loft and dropped bales of hay to the main floor. Then he carried them to the various holding areas before sweeping up and even spot cleaning a few of the stalls that needed it, mumbling under his breath.

It was his job to protect the family. He had promised his father he'd do that, and he never went back on his word. Still, Chip's teasing had stung, probably more because it had hit the mark, and Alan wasn't ready to go there. Yeah, George was attractive—sexy, even—and more than once he'd found himself wondering what it would be like to have the guy.... He pulled his thoughts away from that particular track. Nothing good could come of that line of thought. George was a duke, and he was just passing through. A day or two more, based on the weather, and George would be gone, on to San Francisco, or wherever he decided to go, and all they'd be left with were some stories about the time they took in a guy in a blizzard and he turned out to be nobility.

Even letting his mind travel close to that road was a nonstarter. Nope, he had work to do and a ranch that he was going to make a success of come hell or high water, and that was all that mattered. Certainly not the way George had brought a flutter to his belly and made his mind skip like one of his grandmother's old records just by looking at him.

He had responsibilities, and no matter how much George wanted to run to San Francisco or Timbuktu, his own would catch up with him soon enough. Alan knew firsthand you couldn't run away from your duty—no matter how much he, just like George, wished things were different.

ALAN WAS exhausted. He'd had to get the barn in order because Chip just didn't do some things the way he wanted them, especially the hay for the horses. Once he was done, he loaded the snowmobile and ran out to feed the herd. By the time he'd finished, it was pitch black, and he put the snowmobile away and headed inside the house.

George was nowhere to be found, his mother was in the kitchen, and he located Chip in the living room. "The barn is all set, and all the horses are settled for the night."

Chip glared at him. "I had it all done." He sighed audibly.

"I got you all ready for tomorrow morning," Alan told him gently, because yeah, he was probably being a dick, and he'd done a lot of that work just so he could stay out there a little while longer. "The herd is settled in for the night too, and they have plenty of feed."

"That's good," Chip said without looking away from the television. "George took Daisy outside and played with the puppies. He would have helped you if you hadn't been such a big dick. Now he's in his room." Chip looked up and shook his head.

Alan wasn't going to let Chip get to him, so he went to what had been his father's office and closed the door. There were herd records to update, and he needed something to keep him busy.

A bit later, Mom put her head in the door. "Dinner will be about an hour."

Alan saved the file as she came inside and sat on the chair in the corner.

"Do you want to talk about it?"

"Mom," he said softly.

"What do you have against the guy?" she asked quietly.

"Why does everyone else in this family think the sun shines out of his butt?"

His mother shook her head. "Because he hasn't done anything to warrant this kind of behavior. And you usually don't act like this."

He wasn't going to explain to his mother how George got under his skin without even trying. Alan didn't meet many gay people out here in rural Wyoming outside a dinky little town in the middle of nowhere.

"Mom, I…." He lowered his gaze. Alan hated showing weakness, and his first inclination was to use his butthole cowboy superpower and just go at whoever was trying to get to him. But that didn't work with his mother. She had the antidote, and it was the knowing expression she was wearing right now.

"You like him?" she asked, her lips curling upward a little.

"Now you sound like Chip," he snapped and wished he hadn't, because now she was going to know what he didn't want her to.

"Your brother is a smart young man, and we aren't blind." She leaned closer. "I know what the furtive glances mean, as well as how when you let your guard down, you actually smile at him. So what is it about this revelation that he's a duke that really bothers you?" She half smiled to herself.

"Look, he's got a life somewhere else, in a completely different country, and…." Alan realized what he'd said as soon as the words crossed his lips, and he cringed. No one was supposed to know that he longed to get away from the ranch and this life. Yeah, he loved being a cowboy, and the land he worked was part of him, but it was the only thing he knew. And maybe that was a little pathetic. Everyone knew that Chip was going to be able to get on with his life. He was going to go to vet school and would be able to follow his dreams. Once Chip got a good look at the outside world, Alan had little doubt that his younger brother would spread his wings and fly… to wherever he wanted to go. That was what should happen. But Alan was under no illusions that he was going to escape the ranch. It was where he was destined to spend his life, and not because he had ever made a decision. It was what was expected. He had promised his father he would be the man of the house and take care of the family… and Alan would keep his promise.

"Mom, it doesn't really matter, does it?" He pulled himself out of his thoughts and faced her. "How about this. I'll be nice to him, and I won't bring it up any longer. He's willing to help while he's here, and I'll give him credit for that." It was the best he could do. Because in the long run, it didn't matter what he wanted or what Albert Christopher Charles George Montague Lester, Duke of Northumberland, wanted. Or the fact that he could actually remember that mouthful like it was impressed in his mind. George would leave, and that would be the end. He'd go on to wherever he was heading, and Alan would continue on here.

"I can't ask for more," his mother said. She slowly stood, but she still wore that look like she knew what he was thinking. She patted his shoulder gently and then left the room.

Alan sighed and refused to let thoughts of George creep into his mind.

He didn't know why George got to him this way. And the thing was that Alan didn't even know if George was gay. Something told him that he was, just by the way he looked at him with such naked desire. He shook his head to unscramble his stupid thoughts. George would be gone soon, and then Alan's life would return to normal. He returned his attention to the work he needed to get done.

"ALAN…," CHIP said softly from behind him. "Alan…."

Alan lifted his head and blinked.

"Go to bed. You fell asleep in the office again." Chip yawned, in his sleep pants and T-shirt.

"I will." Alan reached over and turned out the work light, then peered outside. The wind had died down, but the snow was still falling, though much more leisurely than it had been the past few days. "Go on back to bed."

Chip went to the kitchen, and the jars in the refrigerator door jangled as he opened and closed it. Alan stretched and yawned, reaching for the ceiling as he left the office, leaning his head to the side to take the crick out of his neck and back. When he put his arms down, he was looking right into George's eyes.

"I wanted some water. I didn't mean to disturb you."

Alan swallowed hard. George wore a pair of shorts and a T-shirt that seemed one size too small and rode up a little against his flat belly. "You didn't. I was doing some of the records work for the ranch and fell asleep."

George tilted his head slightly. "Does that happen a lot?"

"Sometimes. I have to keep up with the business end of things, and there are never enough hours in the day, so I try to get it done in the evenings." He stood still under George's scrutiny, trying not to squirm. A wave of heat rushed through him, and his breath hitched under George's heated gaze.

"I know what you mean," George said.

Alan didn't roll his eyes, even though he wanted to. "How could you?"

George sighed. "Just because I have a fancy title...." He turned away. "Look, I work hard, and I didn't have everything handed to me the way you seem to think I did. I had to work, and yeah, I have a huge house that comes with the title. It needs a new roof that will cost half a million pounds, and the interior needs enough work to make your head spin. I'm responsible for a small town and a village full of people who rely on me to form the basis of the local economy. I have people who tend the estate's sheep, and others who look after the cattle." George stepped closer to Alan, heat and tension rolling off him. "Somehow I have to figure out how to make all of that pay, not just for my own income, but because of all the other people who rely on the estate."

"I never really thought...."

"Of course you didn't. Most people have no idea. Yeah, I'm a duke, but it isn't like I get anything for that other than a ton of obligations and the weight of a family legacy that goes back hundreds of years. I didn't want any of it, and it wasn't supposed to come to me, but it is what it is. So maybe you can understand why I might want to get away from all that and just try to be myself for a while."

When he put it like that, it made sense, and Alan wasn't too sure what he was going to say. He sat on one end of the sofa, and George sat on the other end. He simply looked at him with those huge eyes that seemed to see right through him.

"I can understand that," Alan said softly.

George leaned forward. "You're going to have to explain that. After the grief you gave me, you can't expect me to give you any quarter on that score."

Alan had to agree—he had been a bit of a dick. "Before my dad died, he made me promise to look after the ranch and be the man of the family." God, that had been a difficult conversation. If he closed his eyes, he was right back there in his father's hospital room, just the two of them. The man Alan had always thought of as indestructible now as thin as a rail, with eyes hollowed out by cancer that had seemed relentless in its determination to take away his father. "I told him I would, and I take that pledge seriously."

"Then you understand having a sense of duty and how heavy it can become." There was hope in George's voice.

"I do. I had dreams of my own...," Alan confessed and shifted on the sofa. "I used to dream of running away to join the rodeo, but I fell off a horse when I was sixteen and injured my back. Dad sat beside my hospital bed for days while we waited to find out if I would ever walk again. He was always there, so I couldn't tell him no. But still, I used to want to be a lawyer. I told my mom and dad some time ago that I wanted to fight for land rights and use reforms to help ensure that the stewards of the land were taking proper care of it. The owners as well as the government. But after Dad died, I had to take over for him. I made sure Chip would get to go to college so he can have a chance at his dreams, and I'll stay here and make sure that Mom is cared for and that the ranch prospers."

"But did you ever wish you could just run away, if only for a while?" George asked, and Alan nodded. He had thought about doing just that. "I know I can't run from my life. There are obligations that have to be met. And right now my mother is more than happy to be the queen of the manor. She understands how the estate is run and the programs we have in place. Some of the programs, like opening the ancestral home, were things she spearheaded." He settled back a little, but his posture stayed rigid. "I honestly think she'd make a better duke than I would."

"I thought about running away," Alan said. "Just getting in my truck and heading west or even east for a while. But if I did, who would do what needs to be done here? My mom is capable of running the ranch, but if I left, she'd need to hire help, which would only make the ranch even more expensive. We're barely making it now, and we might be able to get ahead if we can prove Maribelle's colt is from Rampart. That would buy us a small cushion. But leaving.... Honestly, for me, it was never an option." He pulled his legs up so his sock feet were on the cushions and off the floor. At night they lowered the thermostat to save on heating.

George nodded. "I know I'm lucky in a lot of ways. But I never wanted this. My brother was supposed to take over for my father. Mark was groomed for it from the time he was born, and he loved it. He wore the mantle of authority with ease, and all the people on the estate adored him. He had a vision for what the place was to become, and he and my father were already implementing some of his ideas by the time Mark was sixteen. He lived and breathed his role as duke and took it very seriously." George lowered his gaze. "I really wish he hadn't died, because now I'm expected to be him and to carry on what he would have done. That's what my mother thinks, anyway. Mark would have been so much better at this than me, and I would have been happy to finish veterinary school and open a practice somewhere on part of the estate, be the duke's younger brother, and just live my life." He shivered, and Alan pulled one of the blankets off the back of the sofa and passed it to George.

"Does your mother know where you are?" Alan asked. His mom would worry to no end if he just went off without saying anything.

George rolled his eyes. "Are you kidding? My mother gave me six months to travel and get my head twisted on straight. After her blessing, I took off on my own and have been out of communication for a couple of weeks. I sent her an email a few days ago before all this started and said that I needed more time. I didn't wait for an answer. She'd just demand that I come right back, and I can't do that yet."

Alan couldn't imagine the life George was trying to run away from. "Let me get this straight. You live on an estate… and you have people who help you run it…." George nodded. "And you have plenty of money. Yeah, I get that the estate has to pay for itself, but there's money there too."

George swallowed and nodded again, his eyes saddening. "I sound like a spoiled richie, don't I?"

Alan snorted before he could stop himself. "Yeah. You kinda do. I run the ranch here, and there's no cushion or fallback. If the herd dies, then we lose the ranch. If the horses don't pay and I can't sell them because they're sick or something, we lose the ranch. There's a bank loan that has to be paid that my father took out so he could expand the ranch, but he didn't have enough of a plan. So I have a loan payment to make every month, or we lose the ranch." He held George's gaze. "And if that happens, then Mom, Chip, and I have no home, any chance of Chip going to college flies out the window, and we lose our livelihood as well as our home." Alan swallowed, because those were things he never said out loud. All of those items were in his mind all the damned time, rolling around in the back of his head like boulders caught in never-ending waves. His mother and brother knew about them, so he never had to actually talk about the issues. They were a part of this life, and they all had to live with them... always. "Polo ponies and the like are not part of our world." The words came out more derisively than he intended, but it was a fact.

George rolled his eyes. "You know, you really are an ass sometimes. Yes, I have a string of polo ponies. My father loved the game, and he put me on one and taught me to ride when I was five years old. Mark was so good. He loved the game and rode circles around everyone else. I always loved the horses more. The plan was for Mark to be the duke, play polo, make connections, and be the lord of the manor." He pulled his legs closer, like he was trying to use them as a shield. "My plan was to become a vet and take care of the horses, as well as all the other livestock on the estate." For a second his expression seemed faraway. "I'd live in the town, open a practice, and care for the animals on the estate as well as for the others in the area. I'd have a life of my own, and I could come and go as I pleased." George sighed. "Maybe I'd meet someone and we'd settle down, just the two of us and maybe four or five dogs." His eyes took on the color of the Wyoming summer sky when he talked that way, bright and full of hope, but they seemed to darken again. "None of that is going to happen. I'll live in a portion of the big house now. The majority of it will be kept open as a museum under National Heritage. That's the only way we can afford to keep it with the crippling inheritance taxes." He rested his head on his knees. "As it is, I may have to pay out some, I don't know yet. I have a solicitor who is working that out." His expression grew even darker, and then he lifted his gaze.

"What?" Alan asked.

"The last time I counted, there were eighteen people who worked on the estate in one way or another. That's all those families who rely on me, and then there are all the people around the estate who sell things and run the small hotels for visitors." He shook his head. "Sometimes I don't know how I'm supposed to keep all of them happy." His eyes grew wide and his breathing shallow. "This wasn't supposed to be me. This was Mark. He loved it and he was good at it." George's shoulders slouched, like the weight on them pushed him down. "I know I should just buck up and deal with it. But being away from all that is nice. I get to be me for a little while longer."

"And who are you?" Alan whispered into the dimness of the room.

"That's just it. I don't bloody know," he snapped. "To the folks in the village, I'm His Grace." George snickered. "I hate that title so much. It either makes me sound like a ballet dancer gracefully leaping across a stage or like a priest." He rolled his eyes. "I'm no priest, though my love life has been about as exciting lately, and if you ever dance with me, be sure to wear your boots, because I'll tread on your feet." He smiled, and Alan didn't know what to say. He supposed that anyone could lose their way. Life sucked sometimes. "I shouldn't rabbit on about my troubles. The way I figure it, I have maybe another month or so and then I'll go home and do what's expected of me. I'm not stupid enough to think I can run away forever." He stretched out his legs, and Alan wondered about how George had described his love life.

George was a handsome man with incredible eyes and a lean, sleek body that anyone would love to get to know the feel of. Alan's imagination sure had no trouble picturing what he looked like under his clothes. "This town isn't exactly a hotbed of eligible people either."

George snickered. "You have to be kidding me. A cowboy with those eyes and…." He waved his hands up and down. "All of that. You must have to beat them off with a stick."

Alan swallowed. "Maybe I haven't met anyone who really made me think that they'd want the same things I do," he whispered, letting the idea sink in. Alan wasn't a virgin or anything, but it had been a while since anyone had helped warm his bed, and the last guy who had, had done nothing for Alan's heart. "What about you, Mr. Lord of the Manor?" he teased a little, and thankfully George smiled.

"I know a ton of women who would love to be the duchess, but that isn't in the cards." George's gaze bored into Alan, raising the heat in the room by the second. He sat, determined not to let George know what he was doing to him, but Alan failed as he squirmed before he realized he was doing it. "I won't be marrying a woman just to make my mother happy. I want to be happy, but…." He turned away, looking out the window. "The last guy I dated… he just wanted to be the duke's husband. He didn't see the real me or care about what I wanted or needed. All he wanted was me on his arm like an accessory."

Alan snorted. "So dump him and find someone who sees you." He knew that was easier said than done.

"I did. He tried to cause trouble, but I shut him down. The worst part was that my mother liked Clive. He was tall and had this black, wavy hair. She didn't even care that he was a man, which surprised me. All she saw was the gorgeous face, the fact that he came from the perfect family… and us being together would look good in public." He wrapped his arms around himself, and Alan spread the blanket over him. Alan inhaled, and his head spun at the earthy, clean aroma that billowed up off George. When George turned his head, their gazes met and Alan stilled like a deer in headlights, unable to move and yet knowing he would be better off if he simply ran away.

"God…."

"What?" Alan whispered, still held in George's spell.

"My mother would hate you on sight." And yet he shivered, blinking slowly. George licked his lips, and Alan found himself drawn to him. Maybe it was the enticing scent that he couldn't get enough of crooking its finger, drawing him nearer. Alan knew he should turn away and leave the room, but he couldn't. His heart pounded in his ears, and he felt pulled so tightly that if he didn't continue, the strings inside him were likely to break. He only had one choice, and he drew closer, expecting George to pull away—maybe hoping he would. Instead, George closed the distance between them and slid his warm hands behind Alan's neck.

Alan gasped as he tasted George for the first time: heated lips, a touch of spice and earthiness, mixed with an intense taste of manliness that nearly drove Alan out of his mind. He pulled George to him, feasting on his lips. He tasted good and felt amazing in his arms, but Alan backed away because this had to be wrong on so many levels. The main reason, though, was that it felt right, and things like that never happened to him. "What's happening?" he asked softly.

George seemed confused. "I thought you wanted to…." He put fingers to his lips. "Did you not…. Did I muck up?"

Alan humphed. "I didn't mean it that way." He sat back. "I meant that…." What the hell did he mean, and why was he overthinking this? George was only going to be here for a few days, and he seemed interested.

"Is this a romp for you?" George asked. "Is that what you want? You have been cold and suspicious about me the entire time I've been here, and after talking for a little while… you let loose all your… manliness and…." George waved his hands again.

Alan laughed. "Unleashing my manliness. Like I keep it hidden until I need it." He liked the idea that George found him manly and attractive. "And just so you know, I very rarely romp, whatever that is."

"Then what were you asking?" George pressed as he leaned forward. "You sure seemed to like being kissed." Damn, was that a challenge?

Alan felt his cheeks heating under George's righteous gaze. "So did you. And for the record, I was asking because it seemed fast, and...." Alan turned to watch the snow fall lightly outside the window. "Not because I didn't like it." He shook his head. "God, we seem to be on different pages no matter what."

George chuckled. "We weren't on separate pages when you were kissing me. Only when you stopped." His eyes grew dark once again, and Alan stroked his cheek.

"I can agree with that." He swallowed hard, his gaze locking with George's.

"Then there's an answer for that." George leaned closer again. "Just don't stop."

Alan chuckled. "Do you really think you and I doing... this is a good idea?" It was his turn to wave. "I'm worried if I unleash all my manliness that it might short-circuit something for you, Your Grace." He added the last part to tease, and George shook his head. "I know... I know... I really can be an ass." He'd been told that plenty of times.

"Then stop," George whispered, and he drew Alan forward. This time George kissed him, and when Alan backed away, he surged forward, holding Alan tightly as Alan wound his arms around George's back, falling into the cushions, the kiss deepening.

A throat clearing made Alan jump, and he nearly dumped George on the floor in his haste to sit up. "I did not need to see that," Chip said as he turned away.

Alan groaned as George hastily got to his feet. "Go back to bed, Chip." He felt defensive, and when he got that way, he tended to attack.

"So you and George can go back to sucking each other's faces off?" Chip turned around. Judging by the smirk firmly plastered to his lips, he was having fun with this. "I guess you like to kiss guys you're a pain in the ass to. At least you have a type." He turned away and headed to the kitchen. "Are you guys hungry, or do you only have appetites for love?"

Alan grabbed the pillow and threw it, hitting Chip in the back of the head.

"What is going on?" Mom asked, pulling her robe closed around her.

"I came out to get a snack and a drink and found Alan and George making out on the sofa," Chip said with fake shock. "I think my young innocence has been scarred for life."

Mom swatted Chip on the backside. "Don't give me that. I remember you explaining the facts of life to Marcie Harper when you were eight years old. Then you two snuck off to Connor's place to watch him breed the horses just to prove you were right. And as for your brother...." Alan wanted the floor to swallow him up, but he'd be damned if he was going to give an inch. "He's an adult and able to make his own decisions." Her lips curled upward. "Just remember that the rest of us have to sit on that furniture." She placed her hands on her hips. "Why don't all of you go to bed and we can *not* talk about this in the morning. Am I making myself clear?"

Chip closed the refrigerator door, a Coke in his hand. "Fine." He skittered past Mom, went to his room, and closed the door.

"Good night, you two." She turned and went to her room. Alan figured he might as well go to bed too, and said good night to George, who stood still, his mouth hanging open.

"What?" Alan asked.

"Your mother is just going to accept all that without a bunch of fuss? What about Chip?"

Alan shrugged. "He really doesn't care. He was just being a little-brother pain in the ass." It was embarrassing getting caught, though. George made him forget his better judgment. "We should go to bed. There will be plenty to do in the morning, and maybe we'll get lucky and this next storm won't be as bad as the last one." He reluctantly turned and went to his own room and closed the door, wishing he'd asked George to come with him. But Alan knew his judgment flew out the window where George was concerned, and he needed to keep his mind clear. George wasn't going to stick around, and yeah, they could have a romp, as George put it, but that wasn't Alan. He tended to throw himself into everything he did, and since he could already feel George's pull, that had to stop. This fascination he had with George would pass once he left, and then things would go back to the way they were. At least that was what he kept telling himself as he climbed into bed. But his mind had other ideas, and they were heated and involved a lot more than just kisses.

CHAPTER 5

GEORGE WOKE to insistent knocking somewhere in the house. Light streamed in the windows, nearly blinding off the snow. He dressed quickly and checked the time before leaving the room. He found Alan in the living room, standing toe to toe with a man at least twenty years older than him.

"I knew that damned horse of yours was pregnant by Rampart. I saw the damned colt in the barn." He crossed his arms over his chest.

"So you're acknowledging that he's the sire," Alan retorted, meeting the older man's steely gaze with his own granite one. "That makes things a lot easier, Connor. We'll get a sample from Rampart and have it analyzed to be official."

"You'll do no such thing, and you know it. What I want is the breeding fee," he pressed. Alan shook his head. George figured that was stretching it.

"You know that isn't going to happen. Maribelle got out, but she was found on our land. The real problem was that you let Rampart jump his corral, and if he made it over to my land and impregnated my horse, then that's not my problem." Alan wasn't giving an inch, and George found that sexy as hell. Connor was in his midfifties, George guessed, and he was a barrel of a man, intimidating as all hell, but Alan stood toe to toe with him. That was hot, and George watched the two men do battle... of sorts. "I didn't contract with you, and I never would. And all I need to do is find an acknowledged foal by Rampart and match their DNA. It will show if they have the same sire. Besides, it's obvious that colt is from Rampart—you saw him and knew instantly." Alan grinned. "Just go on your way. Things happen with livestock, and you know it."

"Bullshit. I know you arranged for this to happen. A healthy colt from Rampart is worth a lot of money, and that will mean a great deal to your little operation here." His sneer had George stepping forward to stand next to Alan. "Who the hell are you?" Connor asked with a glare.

"Just a guest they took in out of the storm." He put on his best haughty air, the one he'd perfected around his parents. "You have no standing here, and you know it. My father did business here over the years. I know how things work."

"Hank," Maureen said gently, "what are you doing here causing trouble at this hour?" She seemed to completely disarm the man. He gaped at her for a second, losing the aggression in his eyes. Then he turned back to Alan.

"I won't give you anything from Rampart." Hank turned and pulled open the front door, left the house, and yanked the door closed behind him. George jumped a little when it smacked closed. Then he returned to his room and finished getting dressed.

"He's an old bastard who thinks he can come here and make demands," Alan was saying as George returned to the kitchen. He said good morning and checked on Daisy and her puppies, all of whom seemed excited and active. George lifted one of the squirming pups and held it close to his chest. The little one settled right against him. Apparently they weren't talking about the previous evening.

"Sweet, aren't they?" Alan's deep voice went right through him, and he suppressed a shiver.

"I didn't think you liked them," George said as Alan lifted one of the puppies and held the little girl close.

Alan rolled his eyes. "I like puppies just fine." He leaned closer and put the pup down as a wet stain spread on his flannel shirt. Alan shook his head and undid the buttons, shrugged it off, and put the stained shirt in one of the laundry baskets.

Damn, Alan was gorgeous, strong, with a light dusting of dark hair on his sun-kissed skin. George swallowed hard while Alan got a fresh shirt from another basket and pulled it on. George was instantly disappointed. He set down the puppy and picked up one of the others so they all got a little attention. "Why does your neighbor hate you so much?" There was a story there, he was pretty sure.

"I wish I knew," Alan answered softly. "He's always been that way. He and my father used to fight tooth and nail about everything. The water for his ranch runs through ours first, and he complained that we were taking too much. Then when it rained, we 'let' his land flood. If there was something he could grouse about, he always would. After Dad died, he wanted to buy the ranch, but I didn't want to sell, and Mom went along with my decision."

George wondered about Maureen's reaction and how the wind went out of Connor's sails with just a word from Maureen. There was more, he was sure, but George wasn't going to ask about it.

The dynamics between them and their neighbors were none of his business. As curious as he might be, politeness kept him quiet. "You really wanted to keep the ranch?"

Alan's deep eyes met his. "There were times when I wanted to run away. Yes, I admit that. But then, this is home, and it's all that's left of my father and grandfather. Chip will probably go out in the world and make his own way, or he may decide to come back here when he's done with school." He sat on the floor and opened the gate, and the puppies crawled all over him. "As much as part of me wanted to run away, and as heavy as the responsibility can be sometimes, I still love the place. Maybe if Dad had lived longer, I could have had the chance to go out and see more of the world, and maybe someday I'll be able to do that yet." The puppies yipped, and they all jostled for a place in his lap. Not that George could blame them for a second.

George met Alan's gaze. "Maybe you've got the right idea and I should just go back and face the music, as it were." He patted his legs, and Daisy came over and settled next to him. He stroked her soft fur.

"That's not what I'm saying," Alan said softly.

"It's not?" George asked. "Sure sounded like it."

He sighed. "Well, it's not. Yes, I may have some wishes, but I made up my mind on my own. My mother and Chip were here, but they didn't pressure me. I got to decide what I wanted to do and made peace with the decision." He gently placed the pups back near their mother, and they nuzzled in. George gently stood to leave them alone, and once they were out, he put the gate back in place, making sure they were warm and their bedding was fluffed. "Let's go outside for a little bit." Alan pulled the winter gear off the hooks, tossing George's to him.

"I suppose we can get some work done," George said. He pulled on warm clothes and followed Alan outside into the bright, almost blinding sunshine.

"I didn't bring you out here to work." He turned north. "Look at those mountains and the rolling hills. That is land that I've seen all my life. I know each of those peaks, and I've seen them in my dreams sometimes. Five years ago, I drove over there and hiked up the tallest peak so I could take a look down. I was seeing my home, all of it at one time. And that's what it is. My home. I'm part of this land, and I know it like the back of my hand. Each twist and turn of the creek, the rolls of the hills, the way the rocks jut out of the ground in places like mini mountains trying to reach for the sky but falling short. Even in winter with snow and ice everywhere, I know this land, and I can feel it under my hands and feet." He motioned to the barn, and George followed him inside.

"I think I get it," George said once Alan had shut out the cold. "This is all part of you."

"Yeah. But it's more than that." Alan went to Maribelle's stall and peered inside, and George watched as the mother nursed her child. "See, I went through what you are now, and I came to the conclusion that this was where I wanted to be. There are things that I wish were different, but in the end, I made my choice and I'm happy with it." Alan leaned against the stall but looked at him. "You were never given that choice. You were just expected to step into a role that you were never prepared for."

And just like that, George realized that someone else did understand. "Everyone thinks I should be grateful that I'm the Duke of Northumberland and just accept that and move on."

Alan smiled. "And you just want to be your own man and make your own decisions about your life." He lifted the hat off his head and plopped it down onto George's. "What do you think a cowboy is? At the heart of it, we're people who want to live wild and free. We spend our lives close to the land, but we live the way we want to and we're true to ourselves. I think that's the ideal for us, and I realized in the end that I had almost everything that I could want right here. I didn't need to go looking for what would make me happy, because I already had it... I just needed to realize that."

The hat was too big and wobbled a little on his head as George nodded. "But I don't know what to do. Maybe it's best if I simply go home and do what I know I'll have to do in the end."

"Or," Alan offered, "you cowboy up, call your mother, and tell her where you are and what you plan to do. Instead of hiding, own up to your decisions, whatever they are, and take charge of them. That's what a cowboy does."

George took off the hat. "But I'm not a cowboy." He lifted his gaze to Alan. "You are everything that entails, and I'm just a spoiled rich kid running away because he's unhappy." Alan was right about one thing. He needed to own up to his decisions and face them. He handed the hat back to Alan. "I don't deserve this." He swallowed and left the barn, returning to the house, where he took off his boots and went right to the room he was using. He pulled his phone from the bottom of his bag and powered it on. He ignored the messages and voicemails and dialed his mother's direct line.

"I thought you might have fallen into the sea," she said without any preamble. That was his mother, never mincing words where he was concerned.

"Yes, but as you can hear, I'm fine," he told her. "I'm still in America." He walked to the window, looking out over the snow to the mountains, covered in white but streaked with black where the rock was exposed. He took a deep breath and released it slowly. "How are things there? Is there anything you can't decide?"

"No. But you need to come home. It's time you took your place here. I can run things, and you… well…." She sounded unusually reticent.

"Then run them for now. You love being the dowager duchess." God, she reveled in the role. "I want to take some more time here. That's why I called."

She sighed. "How long will you be this time? How many excuses am I going to have to make?" And there was the rub. His mother loved her role, but she was all about how things looked, and the longer he was gone, the more his absence might reflect on her.

"Not too long." He leaned on the windowsill. "I have some items I need to work through, and then I'll come home." He wished he could just stay here. That was what he wanted. Freedom and a chance to make his own decisions without the expectations of everyone, from his mother to the villagers.

"You should come home now and give up this nonsense. There are responsibilities, and you need to start thinking about how you're going to carry on the family legacy. We are all counting on you to provide the next generation."

George rolled his eyes. "The last time I checked, it takes a woman to do that." His mother was well aware that he was gay. Like so many things, she simply ignored what she found inconvenient, especially when it came to what George wanted.

"Pish. Your brother would have married and had an heir by now. You need to do the same. Your father had his bit of fun on the side on occasion, and you can as well. Just be discreet, but do your duty."

George nearly dropped the phone. First, because what his mother said sounded like something out of a bad regency novel, and second because that was the first time he could remember his mother ever acknowledging that things between her and his father weren't perfect.

Mark, his older brother, was the ideal child in his parents' eyes. He had been born first and was trained to take over the dukedom from the day he was born. He knew what was expected and never set a foot out of line. He was the perfect heir, and George was only the spare. Where Mark got the attention, George played second fiddle most of his life. He went to the same schools Mark did and basically followed in his brother's footsteps because his parents thought that was fair. But most of their attention was lavished on Mark. George simply made his own way and set his own goals, working hard to achieve them because maybe then he could make his parents proud of him. And maybe they were—George really didn't know. Which was sad, now that his father was gone.

When Mark died, his parents just expected him to step into Mark's shoes, lock, stock, and barrel. They hadn't trained him to take over, and yet he was just expected to be Mark and do whatever Mark would have done. Hence the need to get out as fast as he could.

"Bloody hell," he swore loudly as her expectations once again came into full relief.

"Language," she chided. "You know how I feel about that." His mother was all about how things looked and sounded. It didn't matter if they threw knives at each other over dinner, only if they were seen or heard doing it.

"Mother, as you just pointed out, I'm the duke whether I like it or not, and if I want to swear, I bloody well will. And as for marriage...." Her expectations and heavy-handedness almost felt choking.

"I already have a suitable person for you," she interjected, and George felt the walls of family duty and appearances closing in around him. "She knows your... proclivities and is willing to overlook that."

George clenched his fists. "I will not be sold to the highest bidder, and you are not to bring that up again. Ever!" he snapped. "Like I said, I will come home and take over the position as expected, but I will not marry some woman who is willing to sell herself that way." He had had just about enough of this conversation.

"Oh, please. Don't be so—" His mother's accent grew more pronounced as she got more and more snobbishly proper.

"Ethical?" he chimed in. "Decent?" Machiavelli had nothing on his mother. She would do whatever she had to in order to get what she wanted.

She cleared her throat. "Do you want the title to go to your cousin Nicholas?" That had been the threat ever since his brother had passed away. He was next in line to the title, and George had little doubt that his cousin would spend his way through all of the dukedom's assets in a few years.

"That is enough," he snapped as sharply as he could. "I've had enough with this talking about my life as though you get to make the decisions. You don't and will not." He could almost hear her winding up for her next attack, so he decided on a preemptive one of his own. "Besides, if I get married, I'm sure we can make the old dower house comfortable enough for you."

His mother gasped. "You wouldn't dare." The dower house hadn't been used in a while and was in serious need of updating. His mother had an allowance of her own, and maybe the dower house would give her a project she could take on to keep her busy. The more he thought about it, the more he liked the idea.

"You don't think you're going to live in the main house with me and any potential partner I might have, do you?" He figured that would put an end to discussions of marriage for a while. "I need to go."

"Where are you?" she asked, trying to change the subject. She always did that whenever a conversation went in a direction she didn't like.

It was on the tip of his tongue to answer, but George stopped himself. "I'm safe, and I'll call you again." He ended the call and turned off the phone in case she had some way to track it. When his mother wanted something, she generally found a way to get it. He put the phone back in his bag and took deep breaths as he stared out the window.

Deep inside, he felt the urge to run and just keep running until he was exhausted. But he couldn't keep going forever and would need to go home. Though he wasn't ready yet. Not quite.

A knock on the door pulled him out of his thoughts, which was a good thing. "Mom almost has breakfast on the table," Alan said.

"Thank you," George said. "Alan," he added as he was about the close the door once again. He came back inside. "I called my mother."

"You look a little pale. I take it things didn't go well," he said.

"Every bit as I expected." He didn't think he needed to go into the details. "I told her I was going to stay away for a few weeks, and I was wondering if you might need a hand…. That's what you call ranch workers, isn't it? Hands?" Alan nodded. "Maybe you could use one for a few weeks. You wouldn't need to pay me or anything. I could work for my room and board." What he needed was a chance to figure some things out.

"Is that what you really want?" Alan asked. "Because yeah, on a ranch there is always more work to do than hours in the day." He actually seemed to smile, and George's lips curled upward as well.

"Good." He turned to look out the window once more. "There's something about this place that...."

Alan nodded. "I know exactly what you mean." He came around and stood next to him. "The land is life. It's been here for millions of years, and it will still be here long after we're gone. It's part of us, and we're part of it, and yet it will long outlive us. It's huge, and we're small, and yet we can have a big impact, especially if we don't care for it." Alan stayed close, and George bumped his shoulder.

"Are you a cowboy poet?" George asked.

Alan shrugged. "All cowboys are poets. I think it's the land and the way it gets into our souls. It becomes a part of who we are." He turned to George. "Isn't Northumberland part of who you are?"

It seemed like such a simple question, and yet George couldn't answer. "I don't know. See, what we're looking at is part of you because it belongs to you. What I had growing up was never meant to be mine. Dad and Mark used to ride out all the time to meet with the land agents and the farmers. They would discuss plans for the future, and I was never included. It wasn't part of me because I didn't matter." Whether that was true or not, it was how he felt. He leaned against Alan. "I feel more like I'm part of this place than I ever did at home." Maybe it wasn't the land he felt like he was part of, but the generous family who had taken him in during a blizzard and made him feel like he was part of their lives, if only for a short while.

"Come on. We need to eat before it gets cold. Then we have a ton of work to do. The clouds are starting to roll in again." Alan pulled away, and George followed him out.

ALAN'S LAUGHTER drifted over the snow, reaching George's ears over the roar of the tractor as he tried to get the hang of the beast to clear the ranch drive. At least he hadn't gotten it stuck and had only dumped a bucket of snow next to his truck. He was going to have to shovel that away later.

"That's better. Just take it easy," Alan called, and George got the tractor heading in the right direction and scooped up a load of compacted ice at the end of the drive, where a plow had cleared a single lane. He backed away, emptied the load, and got another one.

Chip pulled around him, giving him a little beep as he turned and headed toward town. He was apparently making a run to help at the store for a few hours and get groceries before the next storm hit around nightfall.

George finished removing the last of the snow and returned the machine to its shed, then shut off the engine. It was only when it stopped that he realized how loud it was and how much it vibrated under him.

He climbed down and met Maureen and Alan as they loaded up the snowmobiles with cattle feed. He helped them get the snowmobiles ready, and when they rode off, George went into the barn to check over the horses and make sure they had feed and plenty of water. He also helped clear some of the waste and spread clean bedding.

The snowmobile engines drew closer once again and then stopped. "How is the colt?" Maureen asked as she strode inside.

"He's doing very well. A smart little thing, that's for sure." He was already curiously exploring his enclosure. "You'll need to prove his parentage."

Alan came in as well. "John Vasquez has a colt from Rampart," he said. "I called him the other day, and he told me that he'd let us have a sample from Hercules. He bred his dam to Rampart three years ago."

"I can take the samples and send them to a lab after the storm breaks," George offered. "A colleague from school owes me a favor, and he should be able to expedite the test. Are you really planning to sell him?"

Alan and Maureen exchanged glances. "As much as I hate to say it, we don't have a real choice," Maureen said and left the barn.

George grabbed a few carrots and gave Maribelle a treat, patting her nose lightly. "You're a good mama, aren't you?" She nickered and nudged his hand, looking for more.

"You're going to spoil her," Alan told him.

"That's not possible. Horses are like babies. All they need is food, drink, and love. When they have those, they thrive." He stroked her soft nose once more and moved away, letting her go back to her dinner. "What's next on the list?"

Alan looked out the window. "I was going to try to exercise some of the horses, but everything is so slick and the snow is so deep in places that I don't think it's a good idea."

"We can clear one of the paddocks once the storm passes, and then the horses can be let out." The sun had already disappeared under the clouds. George was used to bad weather—the north of England was famous for it. But they never got anything like these storms, dumping this amount of snow. Usually, they came in as rain, low clouds, and wind that went through everything. But not the kind of snow that piled on for days on end. "They've all been cooped up in here for a while."

Alan shrugged. "It can't be helped."

George began sweeping down the aisles and then checked the tack room, which was a mess. His father would have had a shouting match. Alan looked in on him, seeing his dismay.

"That's Chip's job, and he seems to think that stuff can be put wherever he wants to set it." Alan sighed and began arranging things on the hooks, putting them back where they belonged.

"He's still young and so full of energy," George said and then grew quiet as Alan continued working. "When it isn't snowing and blowing, what is it you do for fun out here?"

Alan shrugged. "There isn't a lot of time. In the summer, I'd go out for a ride. There's the creek with all the trees and shade. I like to go out there when I need a chance to be by myself. When we were kids, we used to go sledding down one of the hills on the property. In town, there's an old roller rink where we used to skate and hang out. Saturdays they held dances and things, but it closed four or five years ago. There's a park in town with a swimming pool that we used to beg Mom to take us to when the summer heat got too much. Mostly our lives revolved around the livestock here on the ranch." He hung up a bridle and paused with his hand on the peg. "Both Chip and I were in 4H when we were kids. Dad always made sure we had steers, goats, or sheep to raise for our projects. They won ribbons, but all that stuff has been put away now." He swallowed, looking like a kid for a few seconds. "I used to love that, and I loved the fair in the summer. I haven't been in quite a while."

"We have fetes back home. Village fairs, as you'd call them. They were a chance for everyone to come together. My father used to kick them off, and he'd sponsor something special to help bring in people and make it memorable. I used to help with the livestock every year." George smiled at the memory.

The wind rattled the windows and then died away once again. "I suppose we should go eat quickly and then get the rest of the work done before the weather turns nasty once again." George held open the door as the wind blew across the snow, lifting powder into the air and swirling it around. Once Alan came out, he closed the door and followed his tight backside toward the house.

"Is THIS really your family home?" Chip asked as he plopped on the sofa that evening with his iPad. George nodded. "It's huge, and look at all the stuff. Are all those paintings and things real?" He seemed awestruck.

"Yes. But remember they belong to the dukedom. They're not really mine. The duke is more of a caretaker, seeing all those things through for the future." He smiled wryly as he thought of the bills that were sure to come for restoration and cleaning. "And think of what will be involved in a few years when I have to replace the roof." That alone was enough to scare him to death. Still, he smiled. "How about this? If any of you ever come to visit, I'll make sure there's a guest room waiting for you." George knew the website Chip was on and flipped through the pictures. "You can even sleep in that bed. Queen Victoria stayed there for a few nights before Prince Albert died."

Chip gasped. "No way!"

"Sure." He caught Maureen and Alan's gazes. "I'm serious. There will always be a place for all of you."

"Wouldn't it be fun to stay in a mansion like that?" Chip asked, flipping through more of the pictures. George knew what they were. He'd seen those rooms every day of his life and listened as the importance of the family legacy got drilled into him and Mark. Well, Mark more than him, but he'd heard that sort of thing all his life. There were entire rooms he'd never been allowed inside because those were the public ones and had to be kept perfect. Pieces of furniture too valuable and rare for him to ever sit on. It wasn't just living in a museum, but in one that he wasn't even allowed to visit.

This is more of a home than I ever had. He swallowed hard as Maureen knitted and Alan watched a rerun on television. "If you'll excuse me." He stood and then went to check on the pups before going to bed.

GEORGE LAY in bed, listening to the sounds of the house: the others moving through it, the floors creaking slightly under their feet, the slight hum of the television. Then, after a while, the house grew quiet and the light from under the door switched out, and still he lay there, trying to fall asleep. He was tired enough, but sleep didn't come no matter how much he wanted it to. Every time he rolled over and closed his eyes, all he saw was Alan. On the tractor showing him how it worked, with their hands brushing together, or the two of them loading feed for the herd. Even in the snow and cold, Alan was a force to be reckoned with. Knowledgeable, confident, and with eyes that outshone the winter Wyoming sky. But what stuck with him more than anything was the look of the man with a puppy in his arms. All day long, Alan took charge, and yet with the pups, he was as gentle as their mother. That only had George's mind circling between their little make-out session and what those hands would feel like running over his bare skin.

George pushed back the covers, shivering as the cold air hit him. He pulled on a pair of socks and sweatpants before leaving the room. The house was really cold, and he got a drink before going to the thermostat, which read sixty degrees—well below the setting.

"It's chilly," Alan said as he pulled an old robe around him.

"I think the heat is out," George replied, turning as the wind whipped past the windows outside. Alan checked the thermostat and left the room, hurrying back toward the kitchen and then down into the basement. After a few minutes, Alan returned.

"I relit the furnace." He raised the temperature on the thermostat, and the heat kicked in. It ran for a maybe ten minutes and then went out once more. Alan got his phone out and made a call before putting it down again. "The gas is out. They're working on it."

"But they don't have a time to restore it?" George asked.

Alan shook his head and went to the fireplace, where he laid a fire and lit it, the flames shooting upward as the draft caught.

"We'll need more wood to keep the fire going."

"It's outside the back door."

George hurried out and found the woodpile covered in snow. He grabbed some logs, knocked off the snow, and hurried back inside. He set the wood near the hearth and got another load while Alan fed the flames to keep them building. After three more loads, he locked the back door and joined Alan in the living room.

"Isn't the rest of the house going to get really cold?" George asked.

"The fireplace will warm this room pretty well, and the rest of the house won't freeze, but you might want to bring Daisy and the puppies in here. It will get cold back there." Alan fed a large log onto the fire, and George led Daisy out, carrying the puppies. He settled her on a blanket near the fire, and the pups nestled into one large pile now that they were warm. Alan sat on the sofa, pulling one of the blankets from the back over his legs. "Come and join me," Alan offered. When George hesitated, he added, "I promise to be good."

George snorted and sat, letting Alan cover him. "I think that's what I'm afraid of."

Alan scooted closer, his leg against George's. "Are you really?" he asked, his voice rough.

George slipped his arm around Alan. "Yeah. On a night like this, in front of a fire, the last thing I want is for you to be good." He rested his forehead against Alan's and smiled before kissing him.

"You know this is a really bad idea," Alan whispered as George settled against him, Alan winding his arms around his waist.

"The last time we kissed on this sofa, your brother walked in on us, and if the rest of the house starts to get really cold, then it's likely we're going to have company in here." George scooted right up to Alan and pulled the blanket up around them.

"Have you dealt with the heat going out before?" Alan asked.

George chuckled. "God, yes. That big estate house that Chip was so enamored of? It's huge, drafty, and cold as all hell in the winter. It has central heating that will keep the place at a moderate temperature, but that's about all. That needs to be updated and replaced too… along with dozens of other things. So you get really good at building a fire in the room you're using and curling up under a blanket." He rested his head on Alan's chest. "Though I don't recall it ever being like this."

Alan hummed softly. "Curling up under a blanket with a cowboy?"

"Well, I've certainly never done that before. But no. Curling up with anyone is what I meant." He closed his eyes and let himself enjoy the crackle of the fire, the growing warmth in the room, and the heat building under the blanket and inside him because... damn!

"There hasn't been anyone special?" Alan shifted a little, and George was able to get more comfortable, his back to Alan's chest.

"Once. Back when I was in school. He was at Eton on scholarship, and then we both attended Oxford. I thought he was a nice kid when we were in school, but university changed him. We started going out as friends, and he wanted to be more. I thought he was special. My mother liked him, of course." George shrugged. "That only pissed her off when I left him."

"Was he just after the money?"

"More like access to my family. Having the son of a duke as a boyfriend and all the doors that might open for him. It got us invited to parties and stuff like that. He was what we'd call a social climber. After that, I devoted myself to my studies. They kept me busy enough. Then Mark died, and my father did as well. Now I'm the duke, and you can only imagine the people who try to get access." He inhaled deeply, surrounded by Alan's warm and masculine but comforting scent. "Sometimes you think something is going to be amazing, and then it turns out to be a huge pain in the arse."

"You never dreamed of being the duke? Not even as a kid?" Alan asked. "There had to be fun times."

"Of course I did. I used to picture myself on a horse in armor, like the knights and dukes of old. I'd slay the evil dragon and save the kingdom. I even had real horses. But being a duke isn't all that glamorous. I have a seat in the House of Lords, which is pretty much ceremonial since all the real governmental work is done in the Commons. I get to see the queen when she opens Parliament the next time. And my father used to receive invitations to royal functions, but I doubt I will. Not that I need things like that. I'd be so much happier if my father and brother were still alive. Mark could take over the estate, and I could open my own business on a corner of it. There are buildings I could convert into a home and clinic, and that would be it." A life of his own for just himself. That was what he'd always pictured. But it wasn't to be.

"There must have been things you liked, even still," Alan whispered as he held him a little tighter.

"There were. We had horses, and I used to ride in shows. I love that. I was really good and tried out for the Olympic equestrian team, but I didn't quite make it. That was okay. I had a good time." He smiled and arched his back so he could look into Alan's eyes. "All my fondest childhood memories revolve around animals… and Mark. He was four years older, but he was great. I used to follow him and his friends around, and he let me join them. If they went fishing, he made sure to pack a pole for me. It was because of him that I learned to ride so well. Mark was good on a horse, but I was better, and he encouraged me. My last memory of him was when I was at a show. My parents were too busy, but he came to cheer me on." George missed him like a lost limb. He sighed. "That's enough of that. I'm tired of whining, and before you say anything, I know that's what I've been doing, and I promise I'm stopping now."

"Life is what you make of it. That's what my father used to tell me." Alan leaned forward, and George found himself kissed within an inch of his life.

"Are you two at it again?" Chip asked, padding out with an old quilt around his shoulders. He flopped into one of the chairs and pulled the covering around him. "Just go do it, for God's sake. Get naked and bang each other's brains out, but do it where the rest of us don't have to see it." He rolled his eyes. Alan grabbed a pillow, lobbed it at Chip, and hit him square in the chest. "Well, the furtive glances and the eye fucking are getting to be too much."

"Knock it off," Alan snapped. "Just be nice for a while."

George stretched out his legs and then slipped out from under the blanket to add a log to the fire. Daisy was curled up asleep with the pups all pressed to her. She blinked and then closed her eyes again when he returned to the sofa.

"I have a feeling it's going to be a long night." A cracking sound from outside made George tense. Alan nearly dumped him on the floor in his haste to get off the sofa to the back door. The lights went out, and the only light left came from the crackling fire.

"What happened?" Chip asked as he jumped up to look out the front door.

"A limb came down out of one of the trees in the yard, and I think it took out the pole. There are lines down in the front yard," George answered from the window.

Alan was already on the phone, talking to someone. "I know you can't get out until the storm is over, but we don't have power, and the gas is out. So we only have the fire in the fireplace right now. … Yes, I know what time it is…." He was getting grouchy, and George stroked his shoulder from behind. Some of the tension eased away. "Just do what you can. I know it's bad, but there was burning out by the pole that's stopped now." He hung up, shaking his head.

"Come on. There's a fire and plenty of wood. We can cook over the fire and heat water for whatever we need," George said.

Alan shook his head. "The water is from a well, so there won't be any until the power comes back on."

"Chip, can you fill a pot with snow? We can put it near the fire to melt. I used to go camping on the back portions of the estate with Mark. He loved roughing it, so we brought very little with us and fished or gathered berries to eat. It was all very rustic until it started to rain or something, and then we hurried home." George chuckled at the long-misplaced memory.

Chip returned with a huge pot filled to the brim and set it on the hearth, then settled back in his chair.

"Should we tell your mother what's happened?"

"If she's asleep, let her sleep." Alan climbed onto the sofa and cuddled George close. "There will be plenty to deal with in the morning. We might as well try to get some rest too."

George doubted he was going to sleep much, and he didn't want to. He was coming to realize that the time here with Alan was precious and fleeting, so he wanted to make the most of it.

GEORGE GREW cold, even with Alan next to him, and he curled up more tightly. Muttering pulled him out of sleep, followed by the crumpling of paper and then a woosh as the flame took. "What happened?"

"We all fell asleep," Chip answered quietly. He fed more wood onto the fire that he'd sparked back to life. Maureen now lay spread out in a recliner, head back, a blanket over herself. Chip added another log, the flames building, and soon the room began to heat. George closed his eyes again, the chill leaving his legs, and fell asleep once more.

At some point, he'd spread out with his back to the cushions and Alan in front of him. The cocoon of warmth was so amazing that he finally fell more deeply asleep, only to wake alone. Blankets adorned both chairs, but Maureen and Chip were gone as well. Light drifted in through the windows, tempered by the clouds and blowing snow. The pan of water still sat on the hearth, so George got up and took it into the kitchen and set it on the stove. He tried the burner, and lo and behold, it lit, which meant the gas had been restored, but that probably did nothing for the furnace, since they needed electricity for the fan.

"At least we can cook," George told Maureen as she came in from outside.

"Good. The boys are going to need a huge breakfast after braving that wind. The barn is warm enough, and the horses have water and feed. Alan and Chip are taking feed to the herd and making sure the path to the water is open." She took off her coat while George fed Daisy and the pups. He took Daisy outside for the fastest doggie potty break in history. Then she returned to her pups near the warmth, and George went to see if he could help Maureen.

She had things well in hand. With her stove working, she cooked up a storm, keeping the refrigerator closed as much as possible. "How long do you think the power will be out?"

"The last time was two days. But with the pole down, that means everyone beyond us is out as well, so who knows. We'll make the best of it. There's plenty of wood. So we'll stay out of the cold as much as possible and keep the herd and horses fed and as warm as we can until the storm breaks and the power can be fixed." She seemed so matter-of-fact. As far as George was concerned, it was a testament to these people's strength. They made do in the face of whatever came their way and took everything in stride without complaining. George let her cook while he brought in more wood and set it near the fire to warm up.

On a day like this at home, his family would settle in one of the rooms of the big house just like the family here had, and they'd read, sit, play games… anything to while away the time. George knew that here it would be very different.

Maureen made up plates, and they took them into the living room where it was warmer and sat in chairs under blankets in front of the fire. They were quiet for a while until Alan came in and began discussing the things that needed to be done.

"I'll see if I can get that generator up and running. If I can, we can run a line into the barn for light," Chip said as he finished his breakfast. "I can probably run a line for the refrigerator as well."

"Do your neighbors have a generator?" George asked.

"Connor has a whole-house system that probably kicked on as soon as the power went out. Dad bought this generator some time ago.

We thought about getting one like Connor…," Chip began, but his words died out, and George got the point. There were more important things to spend the money on, like feed for the horses and cattle. At home, George didn't have to worry about this sort of thing. It seemed rather stupid for him to be worried about the roof of the estate when there were good people who worried about whether they could afford a generator for when the power went out.

"What can I do to help?" George asked as Alan went to the window.

He didn't turn around as he stared out the window, body stiff, looking a bit like a tin soldier. "It's still snowing, but I think the wind has died down some. I sure hope so." He turned back around. "We'll need to clear the drive and get the vehicles uncovered and moved. The horses will need to be seen to…. Chip can do that. The herd will need to be fed. Thank goodness we sold a good share of the cattle in the fall when prices were so good. Otherwise we'd have issues with feed stores." Alan picked up his plate from the coffee table and ate standing up, without looking in George's direction. In fact, he seemed to look anywhere but at him. George cleared his throat, and Alan ignored it. Alan finished eating, and then he carried his plate to the kitchen and got his winter gear on before thumping out back like a herd of elephants.

George sat still, wondering what was going on. Alan hadn't looked at him, and other than talking about the driveway, he hadn't said anything else to him either. George was confused and a little angry. George had held Alan for much of the night, and he thought it was special, even if they hadn't done anything more. But maybe that was just Alan's way to keep warm. The thought made his blood boil, but he wasn't going to run out and ask Alan about it, not right now. He had things he needed to do too, and he wasn't going to let Maureen and Chip down. They were good people, even if Alan the asshole with his cold-running emotions had suddenly made a reappearance. George didn't understand him. Just when he thought he might be starting to….

George shook his head and thanked Maureen for a great breakfast. He fed the dogs and then got ready to go outside. Maybe work would make things clearer.

Then again, maybe everything would be just as muddled as it was now.

CHAPTER 6

ALAN HEFTED more feed onto the back of the snowmobile and ran it out to the herd. This was his third trip. Maybe once the weather broke, he could move them up closer to the house. The field up there hadn't been used in a while. They would have to bring them water, but they would have more shelter and it would be easier to feed them.

Easier…. Nothing here was ever easier. Not the cattle, not the weather, nor the fact that the damned generator had put up a fight before Chip got it started. At least there was a light in the barn, which had minimal windows so it would stay warm, and he'd run a line to the house for the refrigerator and a light in the kitchen, so at least tonight there would be something other than the fire.

The tractor huffed behind him as George cleared the drive. At least that old thing had started. Alan hefted another bale and refused to turn to watch George. He wanted to. The most basic of instincts urged him to turn and watch, just so he could see him. But he wasn't going to give in. Last night had been wonderful, and the thought of George pressed to him was enough to get Alan's heart racing. They had spent the whole night close, with George's arm around his waist. More than once, he'd woken up as hard as a rock and been tempted to roll over and take George's lips and feel his way to heaven. But he didn't dare with the others in the room… and if he was honest with himself, that was a relief.

"Alan," his mother called, and he turned to where she trudged through the snow. "I'll take that on out."

"I'm almost done. You could help Chip in the barn. There's plenty of mucking, and it will be warmer." He wanted the chance to hop on the snow machine and get away for a while. Maybe he was getting a little stir-crazy being in the house as much as he was… spending so much time with George. The guy was leaving, and he knew it. Not that that was all of it. George seemed to see into him sometimes, and that freaked Alan out.

Alan had sidestepped talking about his own romantic past with George, but there had been one person, and Alan had had the same visceral reaction to him that he had with George. In fact, Rusty and

Geroge were way too similar, and Rusty had left him high and dry. The guy had left town in order to get away from Alan, and that had hurt more than Alan had ever wanted anyone to know. He purposely didn't think of Rusty at all. He was gone, and Alan was better off without him, as it turned out. But the whole incident left him second-guessing himself and his own feelings, and that was something Alan couldn't tolerate. His family relied on him knowing right from wrong and what the correct decision was. He had to be confident and strong or everything would fall apart around them. So the fact that George got under his skin in just a few days and made him want things that were impossible for him to have....

Alan swore under his breath as his mother climbed onto the snowmobile and took off, leaving him standing alone outside the feed shed, staring at the snow and forcing himself not to turn around and watch George on the tractor.

"How is that?" George called.

Alan looked up and down the drive, ignoring George as best he could. "Good," he answered and grabbed a shovel to start in on the task of digging out the vehicles. It gave him something to do and a place to channel his frustration. Why couldn't the fates have placed a gay cowboy in his path? Someone who knew his way of life and understood what he had to do. Instead, he got a runaway aristocrat who got under his skin, but would pick up and run off as soon as his old life called loudly enough that he could no longer ignore it. Besides, even if the guy wasn't some duke in hiding, there was very little chance he'd fall for a man like Alan.

Alan heaved a full shovel of snow to the side and then slammed the blade under the next pile of snow to be cleared, lifted the pile, and sent it flying through the air.

"Did that snow somehow get your horse preggers?" George asked, and Alan swung around to a pair of mirthful eyes and wished he hadn't bothered to look.

"This needs to get done so when the snow is over we can get out of here." He was feeling very closed-in at the moment, and the idea of not being able to get down the ranch driveway made him even more stir-crazy.

"I get that." George began shoveling next to him. "But attacking the stuff like it shagged your sister isn't going to get you anything other than a sore back and blisters." He worked along, and Alan eased up, but he still threw himself into the work, if only to keep busy.

Alan was ready to snipe at him. The words were right on the tip of his tongue as he tossed a load of snow. The wind picked up and swirled it right back at him, embedding Alan in a mini blizzard. That would have been bad enough if George hadn't begun laughing. Alan dropped the shovel and lobbed a handful of snow at George, who threw some back. Alan retaliated, and George did as well. Soon snow was flying everywhere, and with the wind adding to the battle, the air grew thick with man-made flurries. Alan could barely see as the snow melted and ran down his face. George took off, lobbing more snowballs at him, and Alan gave chase, catching him just at the edge of the drive. He lost his footing and went down as he grabbed for George, taking him along for the ride.

The scene might have been out of a cheesy movie if not for the rock that had been dredged up with the snow. George yelped and his eyes went wide. Soon red bloomed on the snow under George's head.

"Are you okay?" Alan asked. "George, look at me."

"I hit something," George said as Alan put his hand behind him. Blood stained his gloves.

"Okay." He helped George up, and when he stumbled, Alan caught him in his arms and hefted him up.

"What happened?" Maureen asked as she coasted the snowmobile to a stop. "Get him inside," she added without waiting for an answer. "I'll look at him there."

Alan lifted George and carried him indoors and into the living room, his mother right behind with a cloth that she pressed to the back of George's head. "Can you see okay?"

"Yes," George answered. "And I know what year it is, who's prime minister, and how many fingers you're holding up. I hit my head, that's all." He seemed put out, but Alan wasn't taking any chances, and neither was his mom. She got him washed up and checked the back of his head.

"It isn't too deep, and the bleeding has stopped now," she pronounced. "You need to rest here for a little while to make sure that it doesn't start again."

"I'll be fine," George protested and sat up. Daisy whined and nuzzled his hand.

"You stay here and keep the fire going. It's the only heat we have. If you take care of that and these guys, we can handle what else needs to be done," Alan told him. He flashed George a hard look. Thankfully he took the hint and settled back on the sofa, with a fresh towel over the cushion.

Alan added some wood to build up the fire and brought in another armload, which he set near the hearth before changing his gloves and heading back outside. The temptation to sit with George was so strong, but he had work to do, and getting maudlin and clingy wasn't going to help.

DARKNESS WAS falling by the time the snow stopped and a power company truck pulled up near the house. The men got to work, and Alan's mother brought them hot coffee as they replaced the broken pole and fixed the wires. As they sat down to dinner, the lights flashed on, and after a few minutes, Alan went to the basement and lit the furnace, which roared to life and started its work of heating up the house once again. It seemed the trials that nature could throw at them over the past few days were over, for now at least. The forecast was for sun and warming temperatures over the next week, and hopefully some of the snow would melt away.

"I suppose the water from the snow will help you in the spring," George commented as he sat down on the sofa.

"I hope so. A good melt will help refill the water tables and ensure that the creek runs well," Alan commented. He also knew the higher elevations had gotten more snow than they did, which would mean runoff for much longer. Sufficient water was always a worry.

"Since tomorrow is supposed to be sunny, I thought we might take the blood samples from the horses." Alan was anxious to get the tests run and settle that question. Connor would be upset if the results showed the colt was by Rampart, but there was nothing he could do, and as long as they could prove it, then the bloodline could be documented and the colt would be eminently more valuable.

"Will Rampart's owner give you any more trouble, do you think?" George asked.

"I don't know." Alan wished he knew and hoped he could find something that needed doing. He'd managed to stay out all day and had only come in when his mother called him to dinner. Even then, he'd waited for a while just to give the others the opportunity to eat without him before he came in. Unfortunately, his mother seemed to have anticipated his behavior and was just putting the last of the food on the table when he arrived.

"He may bluster and try to cause trouble somehow, but there isn't anything he can do… as much as he might want to."

"No," his mother said softly as she took the lid off the pot. "I'll have a talk with him tomorrow and put this issue to bed once and for all."

Alan shifted his gaze. "Why would you be able to do that?"

"Never you mind. He's an...." She cleared her throat. "Just never mind. I'll handle it." Alan looked for answers, but he got nothing. She didn't even look up from what she was doing. When he glanced at George, he nodded slightly, as though he might know what she was referring to.

"I'm going to check on the barn," he found himself growling, and he hurried out of the house. Maybe finding something productive to do would help him get this weird twisty feeling out of his stomach.

It didn't work. The horses were fine in their stalls, with plenty of food and water. Alan closed the barn doors and trudged back toward the house under a cloudy sky. Occasional flakes drifted downward, swirling around him after passing the light overhead. The scene would have been beautiful if he weren't so unsettled. The worst part was that he didn't want to feel this way. He should be more in control of himself than this.

The back door opened, and George's figure blocked the light. Alan didn't even have to see clearly to know it was him. The way he stood and how his hips shifted, the way he held his head, the slight movement in his body—it all screamed George. He'd only known the man a few days, and yet even his movements were familiar.

"You should come on in where it's warm," George told him gently. "The wind has died, and it's not supposed to get much colder, so all your charges will be good." He stepped back, and Alan passed him, letting George close the door.

"I got you some coffee," his mother said when he entered the kitchen. Once he got his gear off, she handed him a mug. He thanked her and went on through to the living room, where Chip sat on the floor with Daisy next to him and puppies squirming over his lap.

"We made it through those storms, it seems," Chip said, smiling.

"We got lucky," Alan said. "And we burned through a lot of the seasoned wood." He had put up more last summer, but it wouldn't be dry enough to burn yet. "I'm going to go into town for some more gas for the generator in case we need it again." There was always a lot to do, even when things seemed to get easier.

"Stop acting like everything is the end of the world," Chip said, his mouth drawing into a line. "We made it through two blizzards, and the forecast isn't calling for more." He stroked Daisy as George sat down on the other side of the sofa from him. "Would you consider leaving them here when you go? They're going to need more care than you can give them on the road, and I can find homes for some of the pups. I want to keep Daisy and this little guy here." He held up one of the male pups.

"I tried to tell you this was going to happen," Maureen said softly.

George smiled. "If that's okay with your mom and Alan, I'd like to know that all of them are being well taken care of." Just another reference to the fact that George was going to return to his real life. Alan wished he knew why it bothered him so much.

"They can stay if that's what Chip wants." Alan got back up and left the room, leaving the lights off in the kitchen as he sat at the table. Chip and George stayed in the other room, talking about Daisy and the pups.

"What's wrong with you?" his mom asked as she poured herself some coffee and sat across from him. The only light in the room came from the one above the stove. It was enough to see, but it created interesting shadows on the walls. "You've been a grouchy bear all day, and there's no reason to be. The herd is fine and came through the storm, the power is back, and we have heat. Everyone is okay, and no one is hurt. George was lucky the cut was pretty small." She narrowed her gaze, and Alan brought his mug to his lips to cover part of his face. "Is it George?"

"I don't really want to talk about it," Alan told her. This was something he had to deal with on his own. He wasn't going to talk about his love life, or the lack of it, with his mother. Or the fact that George seemed to flip all his buttons, and Alan really wanted to have his buttons and everything else flipped, in the best way possible.

"I get that. You never wanted to talk about things. Your father was the only one who could get you to open up about anything. Maybe Rusty could, I don't know."

Alan snapped his head upward.

"That got your attention."

"You knew about us?" Alan asked.

"Of course I did. I'm your mother, and I know everything about my children. I know you and Chip think I'm some sort of knitting short-order cook, but...." She smiled, and Alan rolled his eyes.

"We don't, and you know it." She was the one who really kept the family together. Alan worked hard to keep the ranch running, but it was his mom who kept the *family* running and him from working himself into the ground. Without her, this place would fall apart pretty quickly. And his mother could do any of the work on the ranch—and she had, over the years.

She sipped her coffee. "The point is that you and Chip are pretty oblivious to some things. The girl from the drugstore downtown watches Chip every time he comes in the store, and he has no idea. I was surprised when you and Rusty got together. You only seem to pay attention to the ranch and what needs to be done here."

Alan swallowed hard and wanted the floor to open up under him. "That isn't true."

"Yes, it is. But Rusty wasn't the right person for you. He didn't make you feel good about yourself, and you got even more secretive and closed off than you usually are. George isn't like him. He's a nice man who actually seems to like you back, and you're still as closed off as ever."

Alan sighed. "He's leaving," he said softly.

"So? He likes you, and I can tell you like him. You both have a lot in common, whether you know it or not."

Alan lowered his voice even further and leaned over the table. "I'm a cowboy from Wyoming and he's a duke, for Christ's sake. He'll go back to his estate and everything that goes with it, and...." He swallowed hard.

"Okay. So he'll go back. Big deal. What if the time you have together is all you get? What if you and George have a few weeks of happiness and magic and that's all? Do you throw it away or take what life gives you?" She stood up and took her mug into the other room, leaving Alan with plenty to think about.

THE HOUSE was quiet except for the soft hum of the furnace, yet Alan felt something was off. He slipped out of bed and pulled on his robe. The clock read a little after midnight. He opened his door and went out into the hall. Movement in the living room caught his attention. He headed that way and found George sitting on the sofa with a single light burning. "Did I wake you?" He set down the book as Daisy lifted her head from the bed of blankets with her puppies. "I checked on them, and they seemed restless too. I brought them in here with me and they all went to sleep." He smiled as he gently stroked Daisy's head.

"It's all right. We had dogs when we were kids, and I planned to get another in the spring." Alan pulled the robe tighter and sat on the far edge of the sofa. "Are you okay?"

George shrugged. "I often have trouble sleeping. I didn't last night, but normally I wake up a number of times." He sat back. "I didn't mean to disturb anyone."

"I was awake," Alan said. He had barely gotten to sleep at all. His mind had run in circles and wouldn't shut off no matter what. "Though we should move all of them back before the pups need to go." He gently lifted a couple of sleeping puppies, and George did the same. Daisy followed right along, and George got them all settled back in their regular bedding, the pups snuggling right up to their mother.

Alan stood still, watching them as George leaned just close enough that Alan could feel his warmth, and his next breath brought him a whiff of George's sweet yet heady scent. Alan stood and turned to leave as George did the same thing. Alan bumped into him, and George's eyes widened. Their gazes met. Alan expected George to turn away, but he stayed right where he was.

"Alan...," George whispered ever so softly. The words pulled him closer just to hear what George might have to say. He'd used that trick with horses, but he'd never experienced it himself. He didn't move in case George said something more. "We should...."

"What?" he whispered back, his throat dry and scratchy.

George blinked a few times before pulling him forward. "Sometimes it seems you have to take things in hand yourself." Then George kissed him. There was nothing tentative about it. George kissed like a pro, and Alan could barely breathe as he pressed closer. Alan wanted to resist, but it was impossible. George seemed to break down all of his carefully constructed walls, and the arguments he'd run through his mind for days flew out the window at the taste of George's lips and the way his hands slid along the edges of his robe. His skin danced with fire and cold at the same time. Heat and the frisson of cold both ran wherever George touched him.

"I don't...," Alan whispered when George backed away, breathing deeply.

"What?" George asked. "I see the way you look at me, especially when you think I'm not watching." That smile was almost infuriating.

"Still… why would you think that altering everything in my life was something I'd really want?" Okay, so he was being an ass again. He had been up most of the night so far thinking about George. But he didn't have to admit it.

"Because you kissed me like you were dying of thirst in a desert. You slept right next to me on that sofa all night, and because of the way you held me. I'll admit that it took me a little while to figure out what you were doing, but once I knew you were running away and trying to hide, I just figured I'd wait until I had the chance to catch you." George seemed so smug.

"I wasn't doing either. I was busy and had work to do, and…."

George rolled his eyes. "You keep telling yourself that. Maybe one of us will believe it eventually." He put his hands on his hips, cocking his eyebrows slightly. "You know, you can either continue to play this asshole cowboy bit, or you can just admit that you like me and that there's something that keeps getting under your skin." George's voice grew even softer. "Because, cowboy, you got under mine, and I'm not sure how I'm going to get you out again." He shivered, and for a second Alan wondered if he was cold. Then George moved into Alan's arms. "Maybe I have a type and it's cowboys who sometimes act like arses. Or maybe it's just you."

Alan wished he had a retort, but by the time he came up with one, George was kissing him again, and whatever he was going to say died before he could form the words. Not that he was interested in talking at the moment. Alan closed his arms around George's back and lifted him off his feet.

George wound his legs around Alan's waist, and Alan hefted him toward his bedroom. He closed the door as quietly as he could before settling George on his back on the bed.

"What is this?" Alan asked as he tugged at the silk-soft robe George was wearing. "You know you'll freeze if you aren't dressed warmer than this." He smiled and leaned closer. "Or maybe this is just a little bit of gift wrap."

George chuckled as Alan tugged open the knot at his waist, the fabric parting to each side. "You know, this is my favorite robe."

"Why?"

George smiled warmly, his eyes large and beautiful, shining in the dim light. "Because it's the one you took off me." He wound his arms around Alan's neck and tugged him into a deep kiss that left Alan's heart pounding and his ears ringing. Damn, that was something else. George was pretty damned amazing too, especially when he slipped off Alan's robe and pressed them skin to skin, heat to warmth.

"You're a damned tease," Alan said into the darkness. He had to say something, and the way George was looking at him… it was too much. This couldn't be real. No one looked at him with such wonder and care. He looked after everyone else, but George watched him as though he wanted to take care of Alan. It was more than Alan could hope for, but if it was a fantasy, some figment of his imagination, he didn't want the bubble to burst. At least not now.

"I am many things. But I am not, nor have I ever been, a tease." He pulled Alan back down until their lips almost touched. "I fully intend to put out, unless you decide it's too much and go running from the room."

Alan's eyes widened, and he would have huffed and denied everything, but in that moment, with George's gaze pulling him in like a moth to a flame, all he could do was nod and close the gap between them. If he had been a coward for all his doubts and fears, then it was time he put that behind him and followed his mother's advice.

"If I only have one chance, then I should make the most of it."

George tilted his head slightly to the side. "I don't understand what you're talking about."

Alan shrugged. "I'm sorry. It was something my mother told me earlier this evening."

George laughed, a full, rich sound that went right to Alan's balls. "Now you're talking about your mother at a time like this." He put a finger to Alan's lips. "Maybe you should try not to talk at all. I have a feeling that we'll both be so much better off."

Alan wished he could argue, but George definitely had a point. Alan scooted them both up onto the bed and pulled back the covers. George slid underneath with Alan right behind him. The coolness of the room quickly gave way to the warmth under the covers, and this was something that Alan intended to soak in as much of as possible before George left. He hated to admit it, maybe it was better to take what he could get than to deny himself—both of them—the possibility of something magical.

And George was all of that and more. He knew when to take the lead and when to let Alan. George kissed like a dream. Alan had expected George to be gentle, but his kisses were forceful, and when Alan met them, George gave as good as he got, holding Alan tightly, their groans filling the room as their heat built under the blankets.

Alan slid his leg past George's, and George shimmied his hips, making Alan gasp as he ran his hands down George's smooth back and over his surprisingly hard butt. George wasn't afraid of work, and that showed in his body, something else that surprised Alan.

"What?" George asked as Alan paused, meeting his gaze.

"You surprise me, that's all," Alan whispered. And it was true in so many ways. From his strength and the way he didn't back down from whatever task Alan gave him, to the way he met Alan's aggression with some of his own.

"Because I'm not a delicate flower?" George asked.

Alan shrugged. He hadn't expected that exactly, but he also hadn't expected someone willing to go toe to toe with him. Alan liked that. Hell, he more than liked it—the idea turned him on. He kissed George hard, pressing him into the mattress, letting his power take over.

"Did you think I was a piece of glass, fragile and going to break any second?" George pushed at Alan, rolling them on the bed, and then glared down at him, his legs spread on each side of Alan. "Because I'm not." His eyes flared for a second, and then he drew nearer before veering off to suck at one of Alan's nipples. He bit lightly, sending a ripple of passion and lust racing through Alan. George gently pinched the other, adding pressure that damned near had him seeing stars.

"Fuck," Alan groaned.

"You like things a little rough," George whispered.

Alan gasped. "Maybe more forceful than rough." He quaked on the bed as George continued licking down his chest and belly before popping his head out of the covers just as Alan closed his eyes and held his breath in anticipation.

"That's good to know. See, I like to draw things out a little." He wriggled, his smooth skin sliding along Alan's cock just enough to damn near make him forget his own name. "I think that only adds to the pleasure and builds up the tension." He kissed him, rocking gently, and Alan arched up into the sensation. George was driving him completely crazy, and he wasn't sure what the hell to do about it.

No one had ever acted this way with him, certainly not Rusty. He had been content to let Alan do the work. George seemed to like making sure that Alan stayed on the light-headed edge of sheer bliss. "Damn, you are a tease."

George grinned, sliding his hands down Alan's belly and closing his fingers around his length. "I told you before, I am never a tease." He stroked Alan hard with a smile that was pure devilry. "It's just that you and I have all night…."

Alan groaned, because if George kept him on the edge like this all damned night, his head was going to explode. George seemed to relish Alan's passionate discomfort, ramping up his desire with his touches and kisses.

Tired of the teasing—whether George called it that or not—Alan pulled George close. He closed his eyes and rocked slowly on the bed. George didn't fight him, and Alan thrust his hips upward, taking control away from George.

"Is that what you really want?" George whispered. "We can rut all you want, cowboy. Or we can slow down a little." He cocked those eyebrows again, and Alan slowed to a stop. "That's a lot better."

George slipped back under the blankets. Alan wondered what the minx had in mind, and he found out in seconds. His eyes crossed and his breath whooshed from his lungs as George's lips surrounded him. Alan was gripped by wet heat and pressure the likes of which he'd never experienced. He gasped and clutched the bedding as George sucked for all he was worth.

"Holy hell," Alan whimpered, stifling a groan when the ministrations stopped.

"Worth waiting for?" George asked, popping his head out of the blankets. "Then hold on to your head or the blankets…."

Alan barely had a chance to inhale before he was surrounded once again. He clutched the bedding and held on for what turned out to be the erotic ride of his life. By the time George was done, Alan was empty, wrung out, and staring up at the ceiling, his mind blown, along with the rest of him.

"Jesus," Alan breathed softly and tried his best to catch his breath. "You… that…." Words paled, so he gave up trying. George settled next to him. "Give me a minute and…."

George put a finger to his lips. "It's okay. I came when you did. You were so far gone, you didn't even realize it."

"I'm sorry," Alan whispered and gathered George into his arms.

"Don't be. Passion is always the best aphrodisiac, and you, Alan, are most definitely filled with passion." He rested his head on Alan's shoulder. George squeezed him lightly and then closed his eyes.

Sleep pulled at him, but Alan resisted. He didn't want to just go to sleep and miss a few moments of quiet with George. During the day there was plenty to do, but right now… in the quiet… it was just the two of them, and Alan knew that these moments were going to be precious. After all, he wasn't going to have George for all that long. Eventually the rest of the world would come calling, and George would have to answer. So for now, he'd take the moments when it was only the two of them and hold them close.

CHAPTER 7

"YOU ALREADY have the DNA sample from Centauri?" Alan asked as he closed the truck door.

George held up the container. "I got it this morning. Once we get one from Hercules, I'll package it and we'll send them both off. I have a lab that is willing to perform the tests for me. It will take about a week, and they'll give us the genetic profiles of both horses. From there it will be easy to determine if they have the same sire." He had done this sort of work at university, so there was no trouble there. "The lab will also provide an opinion, so that will give us independent verification as well." He buckled his seat belt, and Alan pulled out of the drive and turned right toward town.

"I appreciate you doing this for us," Alan said. "There's a lot riding on Centauri's parentage. There shouldn't be, not really. But the ranch has had some tough years. We're pulling our way out now and getting close to getting our head above water once more. Centauri will mean that we can make that happen a lot sooner and get out from under one of our loans entirely." He continued driving, and George wondered just how close to the edge they were. Still, it wasn't his business, and he was too well-mannered to ask.

"I'm glad I could help out." George smiled as he peered over at Alan, who seemed comfortable—almost bouncy—this morning. "How far do we need to go?"

"Only a few miles," Alan answered. "That's Connor's place there." They passed a prosperous-looking ranch and continued on before pulling into an equally well-managed drive and up to an almost manicured stable area. Alan stopped, and they got out as a barrel of a man came out the greet them.

"Alan, it's good to see you." They shook hands.

"John Vasquez, this is George Lester. He's been staying at the house for a few days, taking refuge from the storm, and he's trained as a vet."

"It's nice to make your acquaintance," George said formally, standing tall. "Maureen and the family were good enough to take in a stranger with a dog and four puppies during the storms. I'm just hoping to repay their kindness."

Mr. Vasquez released his hand. "Hercules is right through here. He's an energetic one, if you want one of us to get the sample."

George greeted the horse, speaking softly, and Hercules came right over, bobbing his head as he sniffed at George. "It's all right." He lightly stroked Hercules's neck. "I've done this before, and it isn't invasive in any way." John stroked Hercules's nose as George got out the swab and took a quick nasal sample before the horse could even register any discomfort. Practice really did make perfect. "He's a beautiful creature," George said, soothing him with soft coos and gentle pats.

"I figured you'd come here," Connor bellowed as he strode into the barn.

Hercules started and backed away into the stall, and the clap of a hoof against wood rang through the space. "You shouldn't snap like that around strange horses," George told him, his tone angry, even if he kept his voice down.

"What do you want?" Mr. Vasquez asked.

"You better not be giving any of them anything from that horse," Connor told Vasquez. "We have business that will dry up if you do."

George shook his head. There were always people willing to try to throw their weight around.

"Just because you have the biggest ranch in the area doesn't mean you get to push everyone else around. And as for our business, we have signed agreements, and if you break any of them, I'll have you in court. My lawyer already has the contracts on file," Vasquez said strongly. Apparently Connor's reputation preceded him.

"Alan here is trying to prove the parentage of one of his colts. He let the damned mother out so she could get with Rampart."

Alan was about to protest when Mr. Vasquez intervened. "That's strange, considering she was found on Alan's land along with Rampart. If anyone isn't able to control his livestock, it's you, and we all know that animals will do what they do with little help from any of us." While they were arguing, George put the sample in a sealed vial and slipped it into his pocket. Who knew what lengths Connor would go to in order to cause trouble. "And the law is clear, so you need to back off. The colt belongs to Alan and his family, and that's the end of it." He narrowed his gaze. "Unless there's something else you want."

Alan stiffened, and it was clear from the way Connor's expression darkened that Mr. Vasquez had hit the nail on the head. "I take it he's after the land," George commented.

"You better believe it. The last three ranches in the area that have gotten into trouble were scooped up by Connor here at near-bargain prices after he ran off any other potential buyers. Rumors start about trouble with the water or contamination on part of the land, and potential buyers run the other way. Then old Connor swoops in and buys up the land just before the bank takes it back."

"Now see here. I've never cheated anyone, and those sellers went into the deals with their eyes open."

Mr. Vasquez and Alan both stepped forward, and Connor took a step back. The two men together were as intimidating as anything George had seen before, and he couldn't take his gaze off Alan, because damn… just damn. "And you never helped anyone but yourself. You're pissed because one of Rampart's colts was born outside your control and without paying you an inflated stud fee. You're cheap and you're greedy. Now I suggest you get off my land before I call the sheriff and have you thrown off. And I'll be rethinking all of my dealings with you and your ranch, as I'm sure Alan will be too."

Connor humphed and hurried out of the barn. It looked to George as though Connor was like other bullies he'd met—basically a coward at heart. "He thinks he gets to run everyone in the county."

Mr. Vasquez nodded. "You'd think someone had made him king or something."

Alan's gaze instantly turned to George, and he shrugged. He knew what Alan was thinking. "I appreciate your willingness to be fair and helpful."

"It's what neighbors do for each other. You know that something will go wrong at Connor's place. It happens to everyone, and he'll be the first one to come asking for help, yet he won't give it to his own people." He curled his lips and shook his head slowly. "I hope your tests come back the way you want them to. Hercules is an amazing horse and one I'm hoping I can breed soon. My son has won a number of roping events on him, and we've been offered a great deal for him. History has shown that Rampart's foals perform very well." He shook Alan's hand and then George's as well. "I'm sorry you didn't see us at our best."

"There's a bad apple in every bushel," George said. "You have some beautiful horses here." He looked up and down the stable.

"You know horses, then?" Mr. Vasquez asked, and George nodded. "What do you ride?"

"I rode dressage when I was younger, but I didn't keep up with it. My father and brother played polo, and they had a string of ponies that they used. I was always more interested in just hunt riding. As I grew up, I became more interested in the animals themselves and studied to become a veterinarian. At least that was the plan. It seems life had other ideas." He didn't think he needed to say more. That was what was important—that, and the way he saw himself on the inside. The title and the rest of the trappings that he'd inherited weren't who he was. George wasn't sure how long he could maintain that distinction, but he was going to try.

He wandered along the stable, peering into stalls and receiving nuzzles and curious glances.

"I see you know your business," Mr. Vasquez said. "Even if these horses have a different purpose from what you're used to."

George nodded. "A good horse is a thing of beauty." He stroked noses and spoke softly to each animal. "And it's what's inside that really counts. Which horses have heart, and which ones look good but don't have the drive." He stepped back and smiled at Alan. "Sometimes you never know. Breeding will only take you so far." George joined the others. "Thank you for letting me see your horses and for helping Alan." He shook Mr. Vasquez's hand again, and they left the barn for the truck, where George packaged up the sample.

Alan drove the rest of the way to town and right to the post office, where George sent the sample the fastest way he could. When he got back in the truck, he found Alan beating nervously on the steering wheel.

"Are you okay?" George asked.

Alan stopped his hands but gripped the wheel until his knuckles turned white. "I got a message from an old friend of my father's. If Maribelle's colt is by Rampart, then he's willing to pay more for him than I thought—quite a bit more. It seems he's been wanting a Rampart colt for some time, but Connor has sold all the breeding shares, and the ones he has, he's… well, not willing to let him buy one."

George smiled. "Then that's good for you, and Centauri will go to a good home."

Alan swallowed and his gaze turned wary. "He'll go to a home where he'll be prized." His words raised George's alarm bells. "Killinger is a good rancher and he raises good horses, but he does it through excellent breeding and buying the bloodstock and lines he wants. I always got the feeling that horses, like the internet business he runs, are like a game to him. Winning and exceeding what he's done before are always the priorities. It's not about caring for what he has as much as just having it."

George understood that mentality and the drive behind it. He'd seen it too many times with some of the people his father knew. It was never about taking care of what they had, but about what they could get and how much they could add to their prestige. Hell, that was how the estate he had inherited was built, so he understood it all too well, but that attitude just wasn't his style.

"Is that what you really want for him?" George asked. It wasn't his place to second-guess the decisions Alan had to make.

Alan shrugged. "Like I said, he'll be cared for, and he won't be mistreated. But...." He sighed and pulled into one of the parking spots in front of the grocery store where Chip worked. "If I could afford to keep him, Chip would love, raise, and train that colt. They would be best friends, and Chip would treat Centauri the way he would treat any of the animals in his care—as though they were the most precious beings on the planet."

George had to agree with that assessment. Chip was one of those rare people who not only loved their animals but understood them. A real-life Dr. Doolittle... of a sort, anyway.

"How are you going to tell him?" George asked, grateful that he wasn't going to have to be the one to do it. He knew Chip was a cowboy and understood these things; he also knew he threw his heart into everything he did, whether it was caring for Daisy and her pups or looking after an unexpected colt.

"He already knows, and I'm just going to remind him of how important our home is. Then I'll give him a noogie, because that's what big brothers do, and the two of us will move on."

George coughed and swallowed to get some air. "You really are an ass." He still couldn't help smiling. "Have you seen the way he looks at that colt? I swear he would have slept out in the barn with him like a kid if it hadn't been so cold."

Alan shrugged. "You were good enough to let him keep Daisy and the pups. Chip is going to have to be content with taking care of them. Granted, it's going to be months before Centauri is able to be weaned from his mother." He groaned. "And months for Chip to get attached."

George nodded. "Now you're starting to understand. I know Chip knows the colt is going to need to be sold if the test comes back with Rampart as the sire, but…." George was worried that Chip was going to get hurt if the colt was as valuable as Alan hoped, but part of him was worried what Alan would do if their hopes didn't pan out, if things with the ranch were as tough as he seemed to let on.

Alan began tapping his fingers on the steering wheel again, and George put his hand on top of them. "It's going to be okay," George whispered, and Alan shook his head before forcing a smile. There was clearly more going on than George knew. "Why don't we stop in at the store? I have some things to pick up for the dogs, and you should message Maureen and make sure there isn't anything she needs." Maybe something normal would help Alan get over this bout of anxiety.

MAUREEN DID indeed send a list, and George put together what she needed and pulled out cash at the checkout to pay. He thanked the checkout lady and said goodbye to Chip before joining Alan outside.

"Even if that colt is from Rampart, you'll never get the money in time," Connor was saying rather loudly. "You owe more than you can handle, and—"

George charged up. "Don't worry about that," he told Connor. "Alan and Maureen will have what they need, and they won't be needing any help from someone like you." He was so angry. George had known predators in his life. There was a Northumberland version of Connor back home. Giles Livington rented parts of his land out for farming, and as soon as the farmers had a bad year, he evicted them and found another tenant. It was awful and very Dickensian, in George's opinion. George turned and strode back to the truck to place the groceries behind the seat. He waited while Alan joined him and then climbed inside.

"I'm not taking any of your money," Alan said as soon as he closed the door. "I know after last night—"

"This has nothing to do with that." George smiled. "Last night was wonderful, but this had to do with the fact that your family took in a stranger and kept him safe from the storm... well, storms."

Alan gripped the wheel tightly. "Look, I don't mean to sound like a dick or to be ungrateful, but I can figure things out. This ranch has been in the family for generations, and I'm not going to let the likes of Connor, or anyone else, take it away from us." His words were fierce and held passion and determination, but his eyes showed something completely different.

"That's all well and good. But Connor isn't going to stop, no matter what you're thinking or the kind of influence your mom might believe she has." He gently placed his hands on Alan's, and he loosened his grip. Alan held them still on the wheel, and George gripped them tighter. "That man is a greedy bastard, and you all know it. Your land would make a great addition to his ranch, and he can probably taste it."

Alan turned his hand over. "I know that. He offered to buy when Dad died. Said that Chip and I could go out and do what we liked with the money. We could be free. But what about Mom? Where would she go? The ranch is a lot of work, but it's our living and our home." The near break in his voice spoke to just how worried Alan really was. "What could I do? I had to make a go of it. I still do. And I have been working my butt off to pay that loan down, and then Centauri came along and I thought that we might have been saved. But Connor is right. It will be months before that colt will be old enough to leave his mother and can be sold. By then... God knows what will happen. We're through the time of year when the ranch brings in most of its revenue. I was able to break even last year and even make some headway, but I don't know if it's enough. Chip is working at the store and doing his best so he can go on to school. I should be able to help him do that, but I can't right now. Yet no matter how bad things get, I can't take your money."

George understood that every man had his pride. He just wished there was something he could do to help.

He wasn't going to push anything on Alan, so he pulled his hands away. Alan started the engine and backed out of the parking space, heading out of town toward the ranch. As they rode, George powered up his phone and checked his messages. There were a couple from his mother, asking him to check in and posing questions about the estate. He answered her, knowing that she didn't really need him but that it was her way to pull him into what she saw as his duty. There was only so long that he could put her—and his duty to the dukedom—off. He hoped that he could have a little more time.

"ALAN," GEORGE whispered. He'd woken from a sound sleep knowing something was wrong. "Wake up."

"What is it?" Alan asked, and then he must have heard the whinny of the horses in the barn at the same time George did.

Alan jumped out of bed, pulling on his clothes as he raced out of his room. George followed behind, jumping to pull up his pants as he reached the back door.

Daisy whined in her bed with the puppies, and George calmed her as he pulled on his borrowed boots, shrugged into his coat, and thrust a hat on his head before hurrying out toward the barn, where the horses were clearly upset.

"What the hell are you doing here?" Alan asked loudly. "George, call the sheriff. 911."

George had forgotten his phone, so he ran back inside and made the phone call, explaining that someone was in the barn.

"We'll send someone out right away," the operator promised in a sleepy voice.

George hung up and rushed back to the barn, where Alan and Connor stood toe to toe, glaring at each other.

"You have no right to be here, and especially not at this time of night," Alan growled.

"It's okay," George said gently. "Let the sheriff sort it out when he gets here. They are sending someone. I think Mr. Connor can spend a few nights in jail for trespassing and breaking and entering." He smiled as he turned to Alan.

Connor huffed. "Now see here, I—"

George stepped closer. "You have no right to be here. None. And yet you show up in the middle of the night and we find you in the barn. Alan, please check around to make sure he hasn't stolen anything or harmed any of the animals or property. If he has, we can add that to the charges."

George was furious.

"I was...." Connor's words slurred as he rocked back and forth.

"What? You're clearly drunk and can barely stand." George went outside and saw a truck parked near one of the piles of snow. "You drove here?" They were all lucky Connor hadn't hurt himself or driven the truck into one of the buildings or the house itself. Fortunately all the snow had acted like a buffer to stop the vehicle.

"Of course I did. What did you think I did? Walked?" He puffed himself up.

George shook his head. "Excellent. We can discuss drunk driving charges as well. I assume that's as bad here as it is in England. They don't stand for that sort of thing there." He nodded to Alan, who seemed to like the idea.

"I'm going, and you can't stop me," Connor said.

"Actually, we can." George crossed his arms over his chest and stood in the doorway. Connor could barely walk, so he didn't pose much of a threat. "You aren't leaving until the sheriff or someone from his office gets here." He was prepared to force Connor to stay, but the man took a step and faltered, lost his balance, and ended up in a heap on the barn floor.

The big man began to sniffle and slowly pulled himself up. "Mary is going to have my guts for this," he whimpered and hung his head. It was pathetic how quickly he seemed to come unglued. "She won't come get me. I know that. Mary told me that if I drank again...." He put his hands over his eyes, and his shoulders rolled as he breathed in huge gasps.

George shrugged and turned away. "There's nothing we can do about it. The sheriff's people are already on their way. And you broke into Alan's barn. What were you thinking?" George asked, hoping for some answers.

"I wanted the colt," he whispered. "I wanted him, and if he was gone, then Alan couldn't sell him and I could have this place. His father was going to sell it to me before he died, but he backed out of the deal." His blubbering grew worse, and George left him to it, standing next to Alan.

The implication seemed to hit him and Alan at the same time. There hadn't been a trailer attached to the truck, so what was he going to do with the colt? Put him in the back seat?

The answer was much more nefarious. He intended to take the colt, but in the bed of the truck, and no one would ever see the little one again.

"What can we do?" Alan asked, getting angrier by the second. The alcohol seemed to have loosened Connor's tongue completely. This little plan had to have been conceived under the influence of a few shots and reinforced with even more.

"Nothing. He's a mess, and it isn't your fault or your problem. Once the sheriff gets here, tell the truth and let him deal with it." George met Alan's gaze. "This is the man who wanted your family ranch and tried to get his hands on it any way he could. And he came here with the intent of harming Centauri."

"But my father…," Alan said. "What if it's true?"

George thought a minute. "I never knew him, but if your father was anything like the son he raised, do you think he would have made a deal and backed out of it?" That was the last thing Alan would do.

"No. Dad's word was gold. Always," Alan said.

"Then that's just the delusions and wishful thinking of a drunk old man. It's what he wants to believe, so it's what he's convinced himself of. There's nothing else to it. And whatever your father might have done or not done, you are bound only by what you feel is right. As you said, this is your home."

As the words crossed his lips, he knew what he had to do. Chatford was his home, and like it or not, he was going to have to return, take over the reins, and see that it continued into the future. He'd always known that, but seeing the determination in Alan's eyes for his home only brought into stark clarity what George had to do.

Those attributes he admired in Alan—his determination, fighting spirit, love of family and their land—only made George realize what a coward he'd been to run away from his own responsibilities. The dukedom needed someone at the helm, and that meant he had to return and take over.

His thoughts were interrupted by flashing lights outside the barn, and Alan went to the door to meet them. After a few moments, he and an officer introduced as Deputy Ransom stepped inside. The deputy helped Connor to his feet and guided him to the car before putting him in back. Alan shook his head as he turned out the lights.

George silently followed him out and to the house, not daring to speak, his emotions too close to the surface. Returning home meant leaving Alan behind, and he wasn't ready for either one, at least not yet, but the time was coming when it would be unavoidable, and that left him scared. What sucked was that he and Alan might have had a chance if their worlds had been a little closer together. But as it was, he could do nothing but pull them apart.

Inside, George took off his winter gear and stepped into Alan's arms. They were still silent, and George didn't need to say anything... not now. He knew what he had to do. The funny thing was—and George didn't quite know when it had happened—for months he had been trying to justify the fact that he had been running away from his life. He'd been trying to get away from the role that he was never born to but had had thrust upon him. George held Alan tighter as he realized that at some point he had stopped running away and started running toward something... or someone. He sighed deeply. Standing in Alan's strong arms, inhaling his rich scent, feeling his muscles shake slightly as they released the tension they held, George figured something out. A sense of rightness and contentment washed over him. He almost tried to push it away, because it would do him no good.

He lifted his head, and Alan's gaze met his, usually so intense but now softer, almost gentle. George stroked his lightly stubbled cheek and tilted his head to the side. Alan closed the distance between them and took his lips in a fierce kiss that threatened to collapse George's legs. Not that it mattered, because unlike anyone else he had ever met, Alan would hold him up and not let him fall. The heat from Alan's kiss nearly overwhelmed him, and George forgot about his worries, what he was running from, and everything except what he wanted more than anything and knew that he could only have in this moment, this instant—because Alan was the one thing he wanted, but knew he wasn't going to be able to keep.

CHAPTER 8

ALAN TOOK what he wanted, what George offered so intensely. Without thinking, he guided George toward his room, and when his legs faltered, he lifted him up and carried him to the bed before closing the door, thankful the others were still asleep. He could tell them everything that happened in the morning, but right now, all he needed was George. And he got him, stripping away their clothes and climbing onto the bed, pulling up the rumpled and now cold covers over them.

Their heat warmed the bedding quickly, and soon all that Alan heard were the soft sounds of George's breathing along with delicious moans that only added to the intensity of what the two of them felt. George was like a live wire, all energy and passion. Alan tried to contain and channel it, but finally it overwhelmed him and he gave up and rolled them on the bed. Lying under George, Alan let him have his way, giving George the control he seemed to need. He was all over the board, and Alan didn't mind in the least. The sheer energy in his hands and lips seemed to take him all in. Alan closed his eyes as George plastered himself to him, kissing so hard and with such passion that the waves George built carried Alan right along with them.

"I never thought I could love an asshole cowboy," George told him with a smile, meeting Alan's gaze for only a few seconds, but with enough heat that it threatened to consume both of them. For a second Alan wondered if George knew what he was saying, but the way he kissed him only reinforced the passion that blazed in his eyes.

Damn, Alan had never expected to find someone who felt that way about him, not in a million years—and certainly not in this small town where he'd known everyone almost since he'd been old enough to walk. And yet his little brother had plucked George out of a blizzard and brought him home... and changed everything for Alan.

"And I never thought...." Alan's voice cracked as he tried to get the words out. He wasn't the kind of guy who wore his heart on his sleeve, and yet with George, he felt it right at the surface.

Alan was the protector, and yet tonight it had been George who had stood against Connor like a damned knight in armor. *His* protector, and the way George commanded the situation had been impressive. Alan held him tighter, stroking down his back, taking in each curve and contour of him.

George stilled, holding Alan's gaze with his own. "I know you find it hard to say what you feel."

Alan cupped George's cheeks in his hands. George did know him, or at least parts of him. He saw things that Alan maybe didn't want to be seen, and yet it didn't bother him. He worked hard to be strong and confident, even when he wasn't. And George seemed to understand that. "It's part of the cowboy way."

George rolled his eyes. "Somehow I doubt that." He snickered. "So you're saying that all cowboys are hot, emotionally repressed asses?" His eyes glittered for a second, and Alan snorted. It was a most inelegant and unsexy sound, but he couldn't help it. "I tend to think it's just you."

Alan shrugged. "I think it goes with the breed. Life out here is hard, and it takes a certain kind of person. You have to be strong and willing to fight. The hard years can be devastating, and the good years are sometimes far between. Most times we work our asses off just to break even so we can move forward. What we do isn't for the faint of heart. My dad used to say that all that hard work and fighting to survive left its mark on a person. And I suppose he was right. We get hard, and we forget about other people's feelings because we just have to do what needs to be done."

"And you forget about your own, I suppose," George said and got another shrug from Alan.

"Maybe they're just less important," Alan said as honestly as he could, then kissed George hard, hoping to raise the heat and the passion because he didn't want to talk about this any longer. Maybe he really was repressed, but he found things like that hard to talk about. His own feelings mattered less than the ranch and how he was going to keep it going—how he was going to keep his family in one piece.

George shimmied a little as he straddled him, sliding his hands over Alan's chest. Damn, George had magic fingers, and Alan hissed and closed his eyes as George plucked a nipple and rolled it between his fingers, sending a little zing racing through him. "You like that?" George whispered.

Alan whimpered as George rolled his hips, sliding his ass back and forth over his cock. That man was sin personified and as wicked as the nights were long. And Alan loved that. George made him gasp and groan with effortless ease, and the way he moved was sleek sexiness on wheels. George had so much energy, and he was so damned giving. As George leaned forward, he held Alan in his gaze. Alan was afraid to move in case he broke the spell that held them both enthralled. George already had him skating toward the edge, and Alan wanted nothing more than to see what the sexy minx would do next.

What he did was blow Alan's mind completely with his touches. George knew what he wanted, and he went for it. Maybe that was the duke in him, or maybe just the cowboy part of George that Alan was coming to see. The man had so many of the traits that the men around here had. Theirs were wrapped in a rough package, while George's was sophisticated and genteel. But all those manners and good behavior covered a spine of steel that Alan could appreciate. "Damn...." He groaned softly, not wanting to wake the rest of the house and yet unable to stop himself.

George had slicked his fingers, and he swirled them around the head of Alan's cock. They didn't have protection. Alan had never bought any because... well... meeting a sexy man in a blizzard hadn't been on his radar. They would need to get some of that sort of thing the next time Alan went into the city. There was no way in hell he was going to buy any from the stores here. If he did, the word would be all over town, and that was not a good thing in any way. Still, George did things with his hands that made Alan's head feel light. Part of him wanted to close his eyes just to revel in the sensation, but he didn't want to stop watching George. He was gorgeous, and his eyes danced with the best kind of wickedness. "What are you trying to do to me?" Alan moaned softly.

George leaned a little closer and slid his fingers downward, ghosting over his balls. Alan whimpered, and George's eyes darkened. "I'm going to make you forget your own damned name." He sighed softly. "You know I won't always be here, but I never"— he twisted his hand, and Alan rolled his eyes—"*ever* want you to be able to forget me."

"That isn't likely," Alan whimpered. Damn it all to hell. He was strong, and yet in George's hands, he turned to complete mush. What surprised Alan was that he didn't really mind. George wasn't going to use any show of weakness against him. Hell, George had his back like no one else ever had and probably ever would again.

For a second, he was disappointed at George's mention of leaving, but then his fingers slipped away and George slid downward, settling between his legs.

Alan groaned. He wasn't ready to play spectator—well, not completely—so he spun George and pushed him against the mattress.

"What did you have in mind?" George asked, surprise showing in his eyes. Alan held him down with a hand in the center of his chest, lips taking in George's nipple. He was lean and smooth and tasted like the outdoors. It might have been winter outside, but George smelled and tasted like a summer day: fresh, clean, and with a touch of headiness that went right to Alan's balls.

George shivered under him, and Alan took a second to straighten the bedding to keep George warm before sliding down under the covers. Darkness surrounded him, but he followed George's scent as it intensified before sliding his lips over him and taking George deep, sucking his flared head and down his silken shaft, taking all of him.

The shaking intensified. Alan worked his hands under George's ass and held him still as he slowly worked up and down and then back up, letting the quakes of desire that flowed through George guide him. "Alan…," George whispered emphatically, his body stilling.

Alan knew George was close, but he wasn't ready for this to be over. He slipped away and emerged from under the covers to take George's sweet lips. He wanted so much more, to be with George in every way, but he wasn't going to do anything that could possibly hurt him. They had to be safe.

George grinned and put up a finger before pushing away the covers and sliding under him, guiding Alan's cock between his lips. Alan gasped and sucked George's cock to the root, using his lips to pull the passion from him. Alan shivered, paying attention to what George did, knowing that guys usually gave what they hoped to get. He mirrored George's actions, and soon enough they seemed caught in a pleasure feedback loop that drove Alan higher and faster than he had ever been before.

George really knew how to give, and Alan did the same. It seemed neither of them was concerned with themselves but placed the other first, and that created a heady experience that Alan hoped would never end. George's quivering muscles told Alan that their energy was too much to last. He slid his hands up along the back of George's legs and then over his butt, ghosting his fingers along his crease. There was shaking, then stillness, and a slight gasp when George came. Alan took all of him, swallowing as his own release ran away with him like a horse with the wind at its back. He lay still, his eyes closed, willing the sensation to go on forever.

A chill broke him out of his postclimactic reverie, and he slowly rolled over and lay on the bedding. George joined him, and Alan pulled up the covers, drawing George as close as he dared. Their heat blended, creating a cocoon of warmth.

Alan sighed and closed his eyes, breathing in deeply just to get the scent of George. He was falling for this man, and there was something that he could only admit to himself: he was afraid. Alan had little experience with affairs of the heart, but he knew enough to be well aware that he was in for heartbreak, and there wasn't a damned thing he could do about it. He held George closer and said nothing. Words wouldn't change anything. All he could do was make the most of the time he had. Then, like he'd done with so many other things in his life, he would have to say goodbye. Alan could only hope that it happened later rather than sooner.

FOR THE next week, things at the ranch settled into a new sort of routine, which included checking the mail for the DNA results, but there had been nothing so far. The sun came out most days, and some of the snow melted. Alan and George made runs each day to check on the herd and make sure they had feed and access to water. In places, enough snow had melted that grass showed through again, especially near the water, where it was warmer. In the afternoons, all four of them exercised the horses. They were happy to be out again. But the best part of the day was after the work was done, the sun had set, and everyone else was asleep. George came to his room, and they spent the nights wrapped in each other's arms. Alan had never expected he could look forward to the nights with so much delight... and growing dread.

He and George hadn't talked about it, but he knew that the time was coming when his bed would be empty again, and he tried not to think about what that would do to him. He was a cowboy. He could handle whatever the world threw at him. Drought, flooding, blizzards, baking heat—you name it. But the one thing he hadn't been prepared for was the way George had worked his way into his heart.

If Alan were honest, he had always hoped he might eventually find someone. He had expected that he would be another cowboy. He'd never expected to find someone like George, who actually saw past his shell to the person he truly was.

"You're so tense," George whispered in the dark room.

"I know." He didn't want to talk about the source of that tension, because that would mean bringing up the subject he didn't want to know about. Alan had come to the conclusion that if George was going to leave, he didn't want to know when. He could go on and just be happy for as long as it lasted, rather than worry about when it would all come to an end. He forced himself to think of something else and to just relax.

"We can talk about it," George said softly.

Alan shrugged. "Why bother? It isn't going to change anything. You're still going to have to go home, and I'm going to have to stay here and run the ranch the way I always have." The fact that he would have to do it alone was closing in on him. These past weeks, once Alan let go of his churlishness and relaxed some of his walls and stubbornness, he had found a person who added light to his life.

"You know, you could go back with me," George offered.

Alan humphed. "And do what? I could work with your horses and be the stablehand." He rolled onto his side. "I can't see your family accepting me into your life. I'm just a cowboy, and you are at the top of society. I don't know how to behave with people like that." God, he would be a fish so far out of water. He gently trailed his hand over George's chest. "This is all I know, and I can't be one of those people in your world."

George put his hand on his and entwined their fingers. "All you ever have to be is yourself. That's all I want, no matter whether we're here in Wyoming, in Northumberland, or if we're in Cheyenne or Paris." He rested his head against Alan's shoulder. "It was you who captured my heart. Not some image of you or some expectation of how you should act. Just you." He chuckled. "Do you really think I'm the image of the perfect duke? My mother wants me to marry a woman so I can have an heir and carry on some illusion that everything is perfect and the family is exactly what everyone expects."

Alan nodded slowly. "And I'm not the image of what most people here think of as a rancher." He held himself together. "I have my mother and brother I need to look after. Somehow I have to make sure Chip gets through vet school, because he wants that so badly. Our family nearly fell apart after my father died, and I helped hold us together and made promises that I intend to keep." Honestly, Alan didn't see how this could work long-term. "Our worlds are so different, even if I can see that you and I are a lot alike. I could ask you to stay here, but that isn't really possible either, and I know that. You have a duty to your family there, and I have one to mine here."

"So what do we do?" George asked.

"You go home when you have to, and the two of us go on with our lives. Maybe you can come back sometime." He hoped that was true. "And I'll try to figure out a way to go see you." God, that was going to be hard, but Alan would figure it out somehow.

The problem was that even as he said the words, he knew they rang hollow. An occasional visit was not going to allow them to build anything. They would see each other and then go their separate ways again. It was only a matter of time before distance took its toll. "Maybe we make the most of what we have right now." That was the best answer he had.

"I refuse to believe that we can't have what we want if we are willing to work for it," George whispered, but with little conviction.

Alan swallowed hard. "I know you think that. But it isn't how things work in my world. I have to make the most of what I can get, and I spend my life taking the lemons that seem to rain down from the sky every damned day and trying to do something with the rotten things. I hate fucking lemons…. But I have to pick myself up and go on, no matter what."

He sat up and clenched his fists. Alan wasn't angry at George, just the entire world and this whole situation. "I never asked for this, but I have to make it work." He settled back on the bedding. "And so do you." That was something he understood. "You can't walk away from your family duty any more than I can."

"So you don't even want to try?" George asked.

Alan gathered George to him and held him as tightly as he dared. "I want that more than anything. I just don't see how it can happen. But I'll do the best I can." He had to give George some sort of hope. Hell, he needed it himself. "I promise you that." And Alan was a man of his word. Holding George in his arms, he eventually fell asleep, but he wondered how much time they had left.

A STRANGE VOICE greeted him two days later as he came in from the barn. "Can I get you some more coffee?" his mother asked in response to whatever was said.

"No, thank you." The man who answered was in his midfifties, with distinguished gray hair and a perfect suit. Alan strode into the kitchen, and the man stood up from the table.

"This is my son, Alan," his mother said, her lips drawn into a line.

"I'm Alistair Simmons. I was sent by the dowager duchess to bring the current duke home." He stood almost too rigidly and spoke with incredible formality. "Your mother was kind enough to entertain me while I waited."

"George is out with the horses at the moment." Alan should have known that this time would come a lot sooner than he was ready for. "He should be back inside in a few minutes. When I left him, he was checking on Maribelle and Centauri." He sat down because at the moment his legs seemed like jelly, and he'd be damned if he was going to look weak for any reason, even if he felt like the sun that had come out in his life was about to go behind the moon… and stay there.

"Is there anything else you'd like?" his mother asked, and Alistair declined with a soft no and an almost regal shake of his head. "George has been wonderful to have with us, and he's become like one of the family." She turned away from the table and put Daisy on a leash before leading her outside. It seemed his mother needed a few moments to herself too. Alan wasn't sure what to say. He jumped when the back door opened and George joined them.

"I probably should have expected that my mother would track me somehow and send you," George said and then smiled as he tried to figure out his mistake.

Alistair stood. "Your Grace," he said gently and then smiled himself. George hurried forward and hugged him. "Now, what are you doing?"

"Alan, this is Alistair. He was my father's butler and the one who kept me out of trouble when I was a kid." He stepped back, and the smile slipped from his lips. "I know my mother sent you."

"Yes. You need to return. There are vital decisions that need to be made, and you must meet with the tax authorities regarding the estate. There are things only you can attend to. The list of things that need your attention is growing by the day." His gaze darkened, and Alan wondered just what George was going to be walking into.

George stood tall, and Alan was damned proud of him. He remembered the day when he realized that the care of his family had settled on his shoulders, and he could almost see that mantle descending on George. They both had known this would happen, but now that it had, Alan wasn't ready. The air seemed to be sucked out of the room, and he knew he had to go with it. Alan nodded at George and then turned and left, passing his mother as she came back inside with Daisy. He pulled on his coat and boots and hurried outside. There was always a ton of work to do, and Alan figured he might as well get to it. The office work was waiting for him too, but he couldn't be inside the house any longer, so he saddled up his favorite horse, Rehnquist, and headed out along the side of the road. There were fences to check and make sure they held up in this snow and... well, anything so he could get away.

The air grew crisper as the sun lowered in the west, and after an hour on horseback, he turned Rehnquist back toward the barn. He'd sped up as soon as he'd seen home. In the yard, Alan dismounted and led the horse inside, where he began brushing him down.

"Alan," George said as he came in. Alan continued brushing, watching him from over Rehnquist's back.

"When are you leaving?" He flicked the brush and then set it aside and moved Rehnquist into his stall, making sure there was plenty of water and feed. "I know he didn't come here just to tell you what was happening back home."

"No. Alistair has taken a room in town, and we're going to be leaving in a couple of days. He's making all the arrangements."

"Is it true you have to go?" Chip asked as he rushed in.

George nodded. "Are you sure you want to take care of Daisy and her pups? The trip home would be too much for them, and I think they'll be happy here with you." That would make Chip's day, but Alan could hardly breathe because all of this meant that soon he was going be alone again. "I have to go back home."

"For how long?" Chip asked.

George hesitated.

Alan answered for him. "He has to go back to his life. There are people depending on him back home. George will be here for a few more days, and then he and Alistair will be returning to England." Taking a part of his heart right along with them. But there was nothing he could do about it.

"That sucks," Chip said. "All of us are going to miss you, ya know that."

"I think I do." George went up to Chip. "You get yourself into vet school, and if you need a reference or someone to give a good word, I'll make sure you know how to get in touch with me."

Chip grinned. "You'd do that?"

George nodded. "What the hell good is it to be a duke if you can't help your friends when they deserve it? Now, take good care of all the creatures you have here, and if you need advice or just to talk through a problem, you know I'll be there." George's voice began to break, and Alan felt his own traitorous throat ache. He buried it as deeply as he could. He had to be strong.

"Thanks, George," Chip said and then squinted toward Alan. "I told you he was a good guy when I brought him home from the store."

Alan rolled his eyes, and Chip nearly stuck his tongue out. Sometimes he was such a little brother.

"Yeah, yeah. Now is everything put away out here, and all the horses set for the night?"

"Of course they are." He smacked Alan on the arm and hurried out of the barn like Alan was going to run after him.

"He's such a kid."

"Thank God," George said softly. "Your brother has this energy, and that will serve him well. He has a long road before he reaches his goals, and that energy and attitude will help him get there." He drew closer, and the heat washing off George meant Alan had to force himself to hold back. The urge to touch was great, but he forced his arms to stay at his sides. "But I'm not here to talk about him."

Alan knew that. "Just a couple of days."

"Yeah," George whispered as Alan's phone chimed in his pocket. He pulled it out, grateful for the break, but as soon as he read the automated message from the bank, he wished he hadn't. "What is it?"

"Nothing you need to worry about." Figuring out how to get the loan current in the next month was his problem, not George's. He'd be damned if he was going to ask him for money. Alan had his pride. He wasn't sure what he was going to do, but he'd worry about it once George was gone.

George placed his hand on his shoulder, and Alan turned, trying his best not to feel exposed. "Is it about the loan?"

Alan huffed. "I thought upper-class people never talked about money."

George rolled his eyes. "They never talk about money when they need it. The rest of the time it's pretty much most of what they think about. How are we going to pay the taxes? The roof needs to be replaced. How are we going to raise that money? The fact that none of the estate can be sold because it's already entailed and listed as historical. Every decision we make comes down to money. But no, we don't talk about such things in polite society." His accent lay thick and heavy, and Alan found his temperature rising. Damn, he loved when George spoke that way. There was just something about a man with that accent. George could be reading an article about the apocalypse and it would be a damned turn-on.

"I'll figure it out," Alan said softly. "The real problem is that Connor was right. Even with people interested in Centauri, and if the test results come back for Rampart as his sire, it's not going to come in time." He was thinking that if he sold the bulk of the herd, he could raise what he needed, but then he'd be selling off the ranch's future. Sure, he'd buy some time, but the wolves would be at the door again a few months from now.

"I have every faith in you," George said softly.

Alan wished he had faith in himself. Connor was off his back, but that didn't change the fundamental issue. The thought of selling the ranch to him turned his stomach, but he wasn't the source of the issue. That was the loan that Alan needed to bring current. Old man Connor was just a side evil brought on by their financial condition. The one saving grace was that since his little late-night visit, he had been very quiet. Word had spread through town fast, and he was keeping to himself.

Alan nodded. He didn't trust himself to say anything in that moment. He didn't want the money and loan to overshadow what time he had left with George. That was what counted. In a few days, he could face the hard truth and make the decisions that he'd have to.

George pulled out his phone and checked his messages before sighing softly. "I have to be in Cheyenne in two days. Our flight leaves the following morning."

"What are you going to do with your truck?" Alan asked.

"I'll sign it over to you. That way you can use it here on the ranch. Unless you'd rather I take it with me and try to sell it when I leave."

"Thanks," Alan said gently, wondering what in the hell he'd done to warrant having a man like this in his life. He could see everything that George was, and he could have kicked himself for being, as George would say, an arsehole when they first met. "We can always use another truck." He stood still, staring at George, memorizing the smallest details about him. The little lines at the corners of his eyes, the way his hair seemed to go in all directions. It was like his hair had a mind of its own and knew exactly how it wanted to lie. But most of all, Alan would remember that smile—the one George gave him when he thought Alan was being an ass and he was about to call him on it. His mother would call it his "It's a good thing you're pretty" smile, and it always seemed to hit the nail on the head.

George slipped his arms around Alan's waist and pressed to him, their heat mingling. At moments like this, Alan's engine usually revved in seconds, but this time he simply held George back and closed his eyes.

Sex with George was amazing. Alan hadn't been a virgin before he met George, so he knew about sex… but this moment was more than that. It was intimacy on a level he'd never experienced. Alan knew he could share anything with George, and that was what hurt so damned much about George leaving. Yeah, Alan might be lucky enough to find someone, but it would be nearly impossible to find what he had with George right now. This was one of those moments where they didn't have to say anything because he already knew what George was feeling, because he felt the exact same way.

Alan closed his eyes and gently cupped George's head in his hands, running his fingers through his mussed but soft hair. The horses moved nearby, and an occasional whinny or huff filled the barn, but Alan just let himself float on George's scent and closeness while the animals serenaded them in the background. For as long as he held George, his world was right where it should be, and he was in the place he was born to be. Alan had to wonder if he was only destined to have that contentment for a few days.

THE EVENING passed in the blink of an eye, but once they went to bed, Alan held George to him and stared up at the ceiling, afraid to close his eyes in case he went to sleep and missed some of the precious hours they had left.

"You know nothing is going to stop the clock," George said softly as he turned over, his eyes holding the same sense of impending loss that Alan could feel. "I spoke to Maureen, and she's going to feed the herd in the morning and watch over things."

"What did you have in mind?"

"Maybe a ride," George whispered. "It's supposed to be sunny tomorrow, and with some of the snow melting…." He snuggled closer.

"We can do that," Alan answered softly.

"Good." George patted his chest and got comfortable. Alan wrapped his arm around him and allowed his eyes to close. They had one more day, and he needed to make the most of it.

CHAPTER 9

IT WAS wonderful to be outside. The air was crisp and cold, but the heat rising from the horse beneath him as well as the bright sun kept George warm enough that he simply settled into the ride.

"You don't seem comfortable," Alan said when he turned back.

"It just takes some getting used to." He generally rode with an English saddle, and the western style was different. Besides, with Alan in front of him, part of his attention was on the view, and what a sight it was. A tight cowboy ass encased in tight jeans. George realized that view rivaled the amazing snow-capped mountains around them. "But I'm okay." He allowed himself to settle and relax. It felt good to be out.

"Are you sure?" Alan nudged Rehnquist forward as soon as he nodded, and the horse took off along the side of the road. George nudged Betty Anne forward as well and easily caught up to Alan, who slowed. "That's Connor's place. We should probably turn back."

They both checked the road and turned the horses around to go home. The ride was pleasant, quiet, and George sank into his own thoughts with no cars approaching down the road. Alan checked the mail on the way in, grabbed the contents of the box, and walked Rehnquist the rest of the way to the barn.

Alan dismounted and took his horse inside while George and Betty Anne slowly plodded down the drive. George continued behind and arrived in the yard a little after him. After dismounting, he found Alan standing in front of his horse, staring at an envelope.

George got Betty Anne in her stall and took care of Rehnquist while Alan turned the envelope in his hands. "I don't know whether to be excited or scared to death."

George closed the stall door and joined Alan. "Why don't you just open it and find out? The answer isn't going to change."

Alan swallowed hard and then handed him the envelope. "You read it."

George slipped open the envelope. He sucked on the small cut on his finger that it gave him and then pulled open the flap and took out the page inside. He looked over the results and read the letter. "Both horses have the same sire. They were able to find a specific marker that Rampart has passed to both colts." He grinned and folded Alan into his arms. "Centauri is a fully healthy Rampart colt, and we now have the genetic profiles to prove it." He grinned, and Alan held him tighter. George knew he was pleased, but he still felt the tension in him. "That should be enough to get the wolves off your back for a while."

Alan shrugged. "Let's hope so." He let out a long, slow breath before folding the letter and slipping it into his pocket. Then he seemed to switch gears and get to work.

Once they had everything put away, George and Alan went inside and took off their winter gear. George stayed behind to play with Daisy and the pups, who were all over the place, little bundles of energy. They were sweet. Daisy seemed the proud mama as she watched over her little ones. As much as he loved the puppies, George had fallen for their mother. She quietly came over to him and leaned against his leg as he squatted down. "You're a sweet girl, and Chip has promised to take really good care of you after I have to go." He stroked her head. "I'm going to miss you." The puppies all rolled around on the floor, with one of them deciding the cuff of his jeans was a chew toy, which meant the others all joined in.

"Hey." George lifted the instigator and stared into her little face. They were all so cute and getting prettier by the day. Daisy looked so much healthier, her coat filling in and her eyes bright. George stayed with the dogs until the pups wore themselves out and ended up sleeping in a pile on the blankets.

Daisy wandered over because she was one smart mama and knew to sleep when her babies did. George gave her a gentle stroke and left her alone before venturing farther into the house.

"Hank is not a problem," Maureen was saying emphatically. "In fact, he's interested in buying Centauri and will advance us the money we need right now."

"What?" Alan said loudly. "What did you do? He wants to take everything we have." The anger and surprise in Alan's voice rang through the house.

George shook his head, wondering what the hell was going on. He got a drink of water and sat at the table, not wanting to interrupt. He didn't want to eavesdrop either. He hoped the sound of the chair was enough to clue them in that he was there. But either they didn't notice or they didn't care.

"Yes, he wanted to buy the ranch, and your father was considering selling. I was the one to convince him otherwise." She cleared her throat. "Like it or not, Hank Connor and I have a history. He's been our neighbor for decades. He started his ranch at about the same time as your father and I moved in here."

"Mother," Alan groaned. "There's something you aren't telling me." George wished he could see Maureen's expression, wondering why Alan came to that conclusion. "What is it? Hank showed up here drunk and was intent on taking Centauri, and he only had a truck. Now you're listening to him and willing to sell him the colt. What gives?"

George stood and put his glass in the sink, clearing his throat because he wasn't sure he should be hearing this.

"Mother," Alan snapped after a moment of quiet. "What is going on? What did you do?"

"I approached Hank, and he made the offer for Centauri." She turned toward George.

"Did you accept it?" Alan jumped to his feet. "Don't look at George. He isn't going to be able to help you. I have someone who is interested as well."

Maureen glared at Alan. "Don't talk to me like that. I'm your mother."

Alan glared back. "And I'm the one who put his life on hold so I could try to save the ranch. The one you and Dad put in such a bad position that I'm still trying to dig us out. I've been working my ass off since Dad died, and you don't get to pull the mother card. Not now when this is so important." Frustration and hurt rolled off him in waves. George didn't know how fair Alan was being to her, but the hurt in his expression told George a hell of a lot.

Maureen looked about ready to blow for a few seconds, and then she sat straighter in her chair. "No. I would never do something like that without discussing it with you and Chip."

Instantly some of the air went out of Alan's sails, and he sat back down. "Good."

George cleared his throat once again. "If I can stick my nose in where it doesn't belong, why don't you collect the offers and give yourselves time to think? Centauri has the conformation to be something pretty amazing. Yes, his sire is an incredible horse, but it isn't just that." He wished there was a way for Alan and Maureen to keep the colt. Centauri could be the start of something really special, though it would be quite a while before his potential could be realized. George had seen some incredible horses over the years, and this little colt had the potential to rank alongside them.

"I agree," Maureen said. "Thank you, George, for that voice of reason… for both of us." She stood and passed him on her way to the kitchen. "We will need to make a decision soon, but not today." She sighed and seemed relieved. It took George a minute to realize that, among other things, she had managed to sidestep some of Alan's questions. Maybe Maureen and his mother had more in common than George thought. "Would you please call Alistair and ask him if he'd like to join us for dinner? I know you have to leave us tomorrow." She turned to Alan. "I have a roast that I want you to do on the rotisserie."

"Yes, Mom," Alan agreed, and George sent a message to Alistair. He already knew the message he'd receive in return. He'd known Alistair since he was a child, and he loved both him and his wife, Helen. They had been at the estate for as long as he could remember. But since the title had settled on George, things had changed. Alistair had become more formal. George was the boss, and Alistair worked for him. George understood the need for the separation, but it only added to the isolation he knew was coming. Just as he expected, Alistair politely bowed out, saying he had arrangements to make and it was best to do them from where he was.

Please tell them thank you, but I'll leave you to say your goodbyes without an audience. And just like that, George realized maybe things hadn't changed as much as he'd thought. *I'll bring the car by a little before nine.*

George thanked him and messaged his mother that he was returning. It was his place to tell her, not Alistair's. Then he joined Alan out by the grill on the small covered porch off the side of the house. "When are you going?" Alan asked.

"About nine," George answered, leaning against the outside wall of the house. "Alistair will come by and pick me up." He swallowed hard. He knew Alan and the family needed money, and he had planned to spend the last few weeks in a hotel. He thought about offering them the money he would have spent otherwise, but he stopped himself. These people were too kind and had too much pride to take it from him. It was probably best if he were to go and simply leave behind the best memories he could, because he was going to take all his back with him, and in the end, that was all he was going to have once he got home.

"Sometimes time is such a bitch," Alan swore and finished getting the grill set up.

Maureen brought out the roast on the spit, and Alan got it going and closed the lid on the grill to keep the heat inside.

"There's no need for that kind of talk, even if it's true," she chastised lightly before returning inside.

George found himself at a loss for words, but he didn't want to go inside either, so he stayed with Alan, just being near him while he made sure everything was working correctly.

The cold worked its way under his clothes, and Alan came over and slid his hands around him and under his coat. "I'm going…." His voice broke. "I'm not very good at this emotional stuff, but things aren't going to be the same without you here."

That was so true. Nothing was ever going to be the same. George's life was undergoing a seismic shift right before his eyes, and there was nothing he could do about it. The wheels were in motion, and he was powerless to stop them.

DINNER WAS amazing, and George made sure to thank Alan for his expertise at the grill and Maureen for everything else.

"I'm sure you'll get wonderful things when you get home," Maureen said.

George smiled. "The cook is good. Mother has had her for years, but she cooks to please my mother, and, well… she has tastes that run a little blander than mine."

Maureen stood to clear the table, and George did as well. He thanked her again and helped out, something he had gotten used to doing here. "You are an amazing cook," he told Maureen. "And I want to extend an invitation to all of you to come visit me in England." He leaned over the table. "And when you do, I hope I can show you the same hospitality and generosity that you have all shown me." He meant every word of it.

"Can I really come visit?" Chip asked.

George nodded. "You bet. I'll reserve the best guest room for you, and I'll take you around the county so you can meet all the farmers and their animals. I can probably arrange for you to work with the local vet if you like. He's a young chap I used to tumble out of trees with when I was a lad." George smiled. "Maureen, I'd love for you to visit."

"Could we have tea?" Maureen asked with a grin. "I always wondered what that was like."

"With decadent savories and luscious desserts. Most definitely. And I bet you'd love riding in the hunt." He'd seen her on horseback, and she was amazing.

George didn't dare look at Alan. Otherwise a litany of all the things he'd like to show him and the places he'd take him would come tumbling out. Some of the things that were on the tip of his tongue were not suitable for the family table. He cleared a frog in his throat and then excused himself. He went to the room he'd been using, but not the one he'd been sleeping in, and packed most of his things.

There wasn't all that much, but it gave him a few minutes on his own.

"Do you want me to visit?" Alan asked.

George didn't dare look at him. "You know I do." He wanted him to more than visit. "But I don't think there would be any need to reserve a guest room for you." He closed his bag and set it on the floor, minus the few things he was going to need before he left. "Look, I want you to come see me and…." He swallowed hard. "You know I want more."

Alan sat on the edge of the bed. "I think we need to clear the air."

"About what?" George sat next to him.

"We're going to be an ocean away, and I think you should try to find someone at home who will love you and can make you happy." The big, strong cowboy lowered his gaze like a recalcitrant child.

George slipped his hands under his legs. "Is that what you want? Me to date other guys?"

Alan stiffened. "Of course it isn't. What I want is for you to stay here so we can run the ranch together. We could build a good life here. It would be just you and me, not the duke and a cowboy, but just us. We could be ourselves and build a life based on our hard work and what we both wanted. That's what I fucking want. But life doesn't work that way all the time. You have to go home because you have a duty to your family and your position there. You can't just walk away any more than I can turn my back on my family here." Alan rolled his eyes. "Besides, what would I do there in Northumberland? I could be the damn stablehand that you sleep with. We could be the duke and dukette." He snickered. "The universe has different plans for the two of us, and it's no use fighting it. And I want you to be happy." Alan searched for his hand and took it, entwining their fingers. "That's all that really matters. I wish more than anything that I could be the one to do it, but either way, you have to promise me that you won't let anyone push you into something you don't want." His gaze was serious.

George stroked Alan's cheek and leaned closer. "You stupid lug. The only person who can make me truly happy is you." There was a price to pay for everything in life. His brother had happily paid whatever was required to be the duke. And Mark would have been amazing at it. But life threw them all a curve, and now George had to pay instead. George kissed Alan and then wound his arms around him and held him tightly. "I know that to be true."

"So what are you going to do? Sit at home and do duke stuff all day? Become an aristocratic hermit?"

George chuckled. "I could ask you the same question." Here Alan was pushing him to go out and get on with his life, and yet he knew that Alan would react the same way to this situation—bury himself in his work and try to forget. But there would be no forgetting for either of them. The way Alan looked at him, eyes already filled with the loss George knew was going to overwhelm him as soon as he pulled out of that drive tomorrow, told him that. "But I already know the answer, and you do too." George squeezed Alan's hand and held his close to his heart. "There's no replacing you, cowboy."

Alan leaned closer, resting his forehead against George's. "I feel the same. You're irreplaceable yourself." Alan slid his free hand around the back of George's head and brought their lips together.

GEORGE WAS packed, and his clothes had been laid out for the morning. He had spoken to Alistair and asked him to get some things in town before he came out to pick him up. He'd given him a list, and Alistair had messaged back that everything was set.

The family was getting ready for bed, and he said good night to Chip and Maureen, then sat in the living room, staring blankly at whatever was on the television.

Alan came in from outside, the back door closing. "It's going to be a cold one."

"Is the herd going to be okay?"

"Yes. Chip and I brought them into a field up nearer the barn, and there's a warming area that they'll congregate in to keep each other warm. It takes a lot for the cold to affect this breed of cattle. As long as they have food, they generate a lot of internal heat." He strode in, looking ruddy, his eyes bright. "What about you? Is everything set?"

George nodded, turned off the television, and stood, joining Alan. He took Alan's hand and turned out the lights as he led him down the hall to the bedroom they had been sharing. George closed the door and pressed Alan down onto the bed.

"What are you planning?" Alan asked, but George put a finger to his lips. When Alan quieted, he pulled off his socks and ran his hands over Alan's feet and up his legs, the skin sliding under his fingers. Alan shivered, and George loved that he could affect the strong man so easily. When he set Alan's foot on the floor, he tugged at the hem of Alan's shirt before pulling it over his head, exposing his work-built body. The sight of Alan without his clothes—or at any time, if he were honest—was always enough to make him forget he was a noble. Since he was a child, he had been coached and scolded into presenting a façade of propriety and decorum. Alan made him forget all that. He was strong and honest, work-roughened and tough, but also gentle, and damn, a single touch was enough to make him weak in the knees. George reached into his pocket, pulled out a foil packet he'd gotten earlier, and pressed it into Alan's hands as a way of telling him exactly what he wanted.

George pulled off his own shirt, not looking down at his less firm body. Alan reached for him, parting his legs as he tugged him close and pressed their skin together. Thankfully he didn't say anything. George's emotions were very close to the surface, and talking would strip away the last of his control. Thankfully, Alan didn't require conversation as he deftly stripped off the last of George's clothes, as well as his own, and pulled George down onto the bed.

Within seconds, his demandingly passionate kisses lit George on fire. He clutched at Alan, holding him as they moved together. Moans and whimpers—mostly his—filled the room, and he gasped when Alan slicked his fingers and teased his opening until George's head was light and he could barely see straight. The two of them had never gone this far, but the rip and fumbling made George smile. Then Alan leaned over him, eyes wide and deep, and pressed his thick cock to his entrance. George gasped as Alan slowly slid inside. He arched his back and held on to Alan's shoulders to steady himself at the nearly overwhelming waves of sensation.

The stretch and burn were incredible, but they paled in comparison to the way Alan looked at him. George got lost in those eyes and let himself ride the range with his cowboy. He pushed away what he knew was coming and concentrated on being in the moment. Alan paused, and George caught his breath. Then Alan rocked slowly, taking George's breath away.

Gasps and whimpers built on each other, and Alan's rhythm shifted, giving George exactly what he needed. Damn, this was mind bending. All George could do was hold on and put himself in Alan's capable hands… and body. Every touch sent him on a journey he hoped would never end. He clutched Alan tighter, probably leaving marks on his back, but he couldn't help it. George felt as though he were going to fly into a million pieces at any second, and all he could do was hold on while Alan rode him for all he was worth.

George didn't know how much more he could take. It seemed like Alan held him on the edge for hours, pushing him forward and then pulling back just enough to keep his head and body from exploding. Then, as soon as George caught his breath, Alan pushed him upward again. George wondered if someone had taught him that or if it was natural talent. In the end, it didn't matter. Alan was a master of pleasure, and this was a ride George was going to remember for the rest of his life. Just when he started to wonder if he could take any more, Alan pressed him over the edge, and George flew into his release on the back of a wild horse running for its life, only stopping when it ran out of energy and was near collapse.

He flopped back on the bed, unable to move. He was covered in sweat, and his eyes drifted closed because it took too much energy to keep them open. He listened as Alan left the room and returned with a cloth that made him shiver. Then Alan climbed into bed with him for probably the last time and encircled George in his arms.

George was afraid to fall asleep but too wrung out to stop it. He burrowed close and memorized each sound, each scent, and the feel of Alan next to him. That would have to see him through the lonely nights he knew were to follow.

ALAN WAS gone and the bed empty when George woke up. Not that he expected anything else. It would be a miracle if he saw Alan before he left, but they had already said their goodbyes, silently, last night... making love. Neither of them had said the words, and he was grateful for that. Without saying those three little words, maybe George could leave with a small part of his heart intact.

"Are you going?" Maureen asked, giving him a hug. "You know you're welcome here any time, and I will come see you." She wiped the corners of her eyes as she pulled back and then put her hands on his shoulders. "Remember us, and you be your own man. No matter what anyone else thinks you should do, make your own decisions and do what's right for you." She hugged him again and then turned to leave the kitchen.

"Take care of Daisy and those pups," George told Chip. "You have everything it takes to be a great vet. All you've got to do is work at it." He hugged the kid as well and then carried his bags to the door, where he gave the dog and each of the puppies some loving before taking his case outside. Alistair had pulled in, and he hurried over and placed George's bag in the car.

"Are you ready, sir?" he said gently. "I unloaded the bags of puppy and dog food you asked me to get."

"Almost." George scanned the landscape for Alan. He knew he'd be around somewhere, but there was no sign of him. "I'll be right back." He went inside and pulled an envelope out of his inside pocket. He handed it to Maureen. He should have given it to her earlier, but he'd forgotten.

"What's this?" she asked.

"Everything you need to know," he told her. Then he left the house for the final time and got into the car. Maybe Alan was right and it was easier this way, but he would have liked to see him one last time. Still, he couldn't make Alan appear, and he got into the car. "We can go," he said softly, and Alistair turned the car around and pulled out of the drive, then made the turn toward the highway.

As Alistair slowed at the corner, a lone rider appeared from between two rises. George knew it was Alan on Rehnquist, with his coat and hat making him appear dark against the snow. He watched, raising his hand as Alan did, and then the landscape closed around him and Alan was gone.

NEARLY A DAY later, on a British Airways flight over the Atlantic, George shifted in his first-class mini compartment. He knew he should sleep, but it refused to come. His body was still on Mountain time, and even though it was dark, he knew it was too early. George got his bag and fished around inside for a book, but he came up with an envelope instead.

"What's this?" he asked himself. It had his name on it. He lifted the flap and pulled out the pages inside. The handwritten script appeared shaky but readable.

George

I knew if I stayed to see you off, I would never be able to keep from telling you not to go, and that was the last thing either of us needed. Call me a coward if you like, but I couldn't stand there in the yard and just watch you go. You have to do what you need to, just as I do. But that doesn't make the parting any easier or the fact that your life is taking you away from me any less unfair. I used to wonder if there was anyone out there for me. And now I know that there is. The fact that he's thousands of miles away is less important than knowing that you are out there.

There are things that I wish I could say to you, but you know that words aren't my strong suit. It's easier for me to be an asshole than it is to just say what I feel. As I write this, I'm standing outside the door to the room we have shared, with the paper against the wall, because I don't want to let you out of my sight during these last precious hours. But I have to try to say what I feel, and maybe it will be easier to write it. I don't have flowery words, and I sure as hell am not poetic in any way. But you already know that. So here it goes.

I love you, George.

I think it happened when you helped Maribelle give birth without a moment's hesitation, but I knew it the moment you stood up to Connor and basically told him to go to hell. That somehow we would figure things out and that I didn't need his help. In that moment, I knew that you understood me in a way few people did. And what's more, you knew that in that moment what I needed most was to know that someone had my back. And I'm glad that someone was you. My biggest regret is that I won't be there to return the favor when you need it.

I'm sure our feelings will change. Distance and time will take their inevitable toll on our feelings, but I will never regret what we had together and will remember you forever. You will always have a place in my heart that I will hold dear to me. Okay, so maybe I did manage to get just a little poetic, and that's because of you too.

Remember that, no matter where you are or what happens, you are loved... even if from far away.

Alan

George's throat ached as he folded the pages and put them back in the envelope. Then he turned out the light and pulled the thin blanket up over his head so no one would see him fall to pieces.

CHAPTER 10

ALAN WORKED, worried, and thought about George nearly every hour of the day for the next week. He was no closer to figuring out how he was going to bring that loan current, and his mother's news that Connor was willing to pay part up front for Centauri was looking better and better, even if the idea set his teeth on edge. Still, the ranch needed to survive, and he had to keep his ego and pride out of it. Though he still figured Connor would try something underhanded.

"We need to make some decisions," Mom said when Alan came in well after dark, his body exhausted but his mind still going in circles. "We can't put this off anymore." She sat at the table and pushed a plate across to where Alan pulled out a chair.

"I know." Suddenly his appetite seemed to fly out the window. Still, he knew he'd need his strength, so he forced himself to eat, even if the food tasted like ash.

Alan called Chip, and he joined them at the table after grabbing a Coke out of the fridge.

"Hank Connor has raised his offer, and I think it's generous," she told them. "And he'll take Maribelle as well, and he added a fair price for her. That way we can move both mother and foal over to his place and we can complete the sale in full." She seemed pleased. Alan swallowed down a mixture of food and bile before drinking his coffee. "In exchange, we'll drop the charges against him for breaking into the barn. Hank will still have to answer for driving drunk, but that's his problem, not ours." Her eyes were clear and her jaw set. "This will wipe the slate clean between all of us."

Alan dropped his fork. "How did you get him to agree to all this?" He sipped his coffee and let the food settle. He got the feeling that there was more than his mother was saying.

"What aren't you telling us?" Chip asked. "Hank Connor never did anything for anyone without something in it for himself."

"That's not true. Hank Connor was a different person when he was younger." She shifted in the chair, and Alan wondered if she was ever going to own up to whatever she'd been keeping a secret. "He was good-looking and rode rodeo." Alan knew that look. He'd seen it between his parents a million times.

"Did you date him?" Alan asked.

His mother nodded. "He and I were high school sweethearts. He was the rodeo king, and I was the belle of the ball. We were in love, and…." She lowered her gaze slightly. "I ended up pregnant. Hank asked me to marry him, and I almost said yes. But I couldn't. Then walls around me began to close in, and I had lost control of everything. Our parents were taking charge, telling both of us what we were going to do and how we were going to act. Hank wouldn't stand up to his father, but I told your grandpa no. He was furious and said I was going to marry the boy that had ruined me."

Alan swallowed hard. "Are you telling me that Hank Connor is my father?" The idea nearly made him sick. To be related to that man…. He shivered.

His mother shook her head. "Oh no. You are your father's son. And I can prove it, because you look just like him. See, I lost the baby, and I stuck to my guns and didn't marry Hank. He was heartbroken, but I had things I wanted to do in my life. So I joined the rodeo as a barrel racer, and that's where I met your father. He and I married, and eventually Hank married Mary."

"But he always carried a torch for you," Chip supplied, and his mother nodded.

"After your father died, he started coming around again, even offered to leave Mary for me, but I'm not interested in getting married again, and whatever I once felt for Hank was long replaced by your father. He was something else, and there's no way anyone can take his place." Color rose in her cheeks.

"But they're still married," Alan said.

"Yes, and Mary doesn't know what Hank offered to do, and I won't tell her. And I won't let her hear anything bad against Hank, but I got him to raise his offer for old times' sake, and he and I can let the past stay in the past."

Alan humphed, and his mother glared at him. "Now, if you'll let me finish. As I said, Hank has upped his offer, and it seems Killinger is interested in the colt as well. But I have a third offer here." She placed an envelope on the table. "This one is for five thousand dollars more than

Hank's or Killinger's offer. Centauri would stay here with his mother until he's weaned and safe to travel, and then he'll be sent to his new owner." She was being cagey.

"Where?" Chip asked. "Mother...." For a second Chip sounded just like their father.

"England," she answered softly.

Alan pushed away his plate and jumped to his feet. "That son of a bitch." He stared at Chip and then turned to his mother. "You have to be kidding me." He should have known. "When did George do this?"

"He gave me the offer in writing just before he left." She patted the envelope. "His intention is to add him to his family stables and put him into training for either flat racing or steeplechase. But either way, he says that he will pay us up front for the colt as well as pay for his board until he's old enough to travel."

"I told him that I wasn't going to take his money." Alan figured this was George's way of getting around him.

"You aren't. *We* are. This is a legitimate offer. George made it very clear that he thinks Centauri is an exceptional colt, and he's willing to take a chance in buying him now, hoping he has potential." Alan knew that look. "I think you need to let go of some of your pride and realize that this is the best outcome we can hope for. George will own Centauri, and we will have the money to pay off that loan and give ourselves some breathing room... and a chance to build the ranch back up again. And we will have that because of George."

Damn. He should have known George would do something like that. He lowered his gaze and took another bite of pork before pushing the plate away. Now he wasn't hungry for a completely different reason. Once again, George had been there for them, saving the day, but this time he wasn't around so Alan could thank him. And hell, Alan missed him like a lost limb.

"If we're all in agreement, I'll contact the person he gave me and arrange to complete the deal." She smiled, and Chip practically floated out of the room. He put a lead on Daisy and took her outside, most likely to the barn. "And you, my eldest son... you need to figure out what it is you want."

Alan shrugged. "I know what I want and what I have to do."

Mom patted his hand like she was humoring him. "If you say so."

Alan shook his head. There was no arguing with his mother when she got the idea that she was some sage who could see into the future and around walls, even if they were the ones he'd built to keep himself from falling to pieces. "I'm fine, and there's plenty of work to get done around here. Now that we have the loan situation resolved, we can arrange to purchase some calves and build up the herd again come spring."

Now it was her turn to shake her head. "I know about all that, and I'm making arrangements. What I want to talk about is you. After your father died, you figured you needed to take over and run the ranch, step into his shoes, and maybe you did. I was in no shape to step in and take over." Color rose in her cheeks and her eyes watered, but she wiped the tears away. "I loved your father with all my heart, and it nearly killed me when I lost him. I think I retreated into myself, and you just stepped up... because you're your father's son. And I let you take on everything because it was easier for me, and I just wasn't able to." Her eyes became clearer, and she sat up straighter. "But the time has come for me to stop hiding behind my loss and step up the way I should have years ago. This land is part of our family legacy, but none of my children should feel chained to it."

"Mom, I—" Alan began, but she cut him off with a look.

"Don't hand me a load of crap and try to tell me it's flowers. I saw you and George together, and I know you. I know you'll stay here and run the ranch because you think it's what you have to do for the family. But you don't. It's time I took over the ranch and stepped back out into the world. And you need to do the same. Stop hiding behind your duty." She leaned closer. "I'll ask you again. What is it you want to do? This ranch isn't going anywhere, and I can do what needs to be done. I think it's time for you to decide what it is that you want."

Alan got up and refilled his mug. "I need to run the ranch. You can't do this alone."

"I can do anything I set my mind to. And yes, after your father died, it was hard. This ranch is our home, but it shouldn't be an anchor around any of my children's necks. Your father would hate to see that, and so do I. Maybe it's time you decided what it was you really wanted instead of just doing what you think you have to."

She left the room, and Alan sat back down, wondering what the hell was going on.

ALAN FOUND Chip in the barn a while later, Daisy wandering around. "You should take her inside to the puppies." It was about time for them to be weaned, but it hadn't happened yet.

"Do we really get to keep him until he's old enough to travel?" Chip asked, watching Maribelle and Centauri in their stall.

"Yes. But don't get attached. He will be going away eventually. As everyone seems to." He leaned on the wall, watching mother and child.

"You just think that because you're still buttsore George left." Sometimes Chip's arrows were too on point for his own good. "And now you're unhappy." Chip gave Maribelle a few carrots.

"Yeah. So...?" he challenged.

Chip pulled his hand back. "So... what are you going to do about it? I'm going to school in the fall, and I'll be gone. I'm hoping for a chance to work in a veterinary office and get some practical experience. Which means I'm not going to be coming home all that often. Mom has decided that she's going to take over more of the job of running this place. You know she did a lot of it when Dad was alive." He sat down on a stack of hay bales.

"And your point is?" Alan asked.

"That everyone is moving on with their lives. It was hard for Mom to lose Dad, but she's coming out of it, and she can run the ranch on her own. She'll need to hire some help, but that can be arranged. I'm going on to school, and I'm going to go and figure out my own life." Chip met his gaze. "Maybe it's time you did the same thing."

"That's what Mom said. But...." Alan stopped himself. "What the hell am I going to do? This is all I know. I had to hold this place together all those months. Am I supposed to just walk away and, what...? Do what?"

Chip scoffed. "How the hell am I supposed to know? Join the rodeo if you want. You could join that troop of guys that came to Casper a few weeks ago. They were cowboy strippers, taking it off for the ladies." He wasn't serious. "Or maybe you could stop acting like someone just took away your favorite toy and get on with it. Do something, because having you around is getting depressing. You work, you mope, and you've treated everyone like shit since George left." He stood and shook Alan's shoulder. "Snap the hell out of it and do something about it... unless you didn't love George after all."

"Where do you get off saying shit like that? You don't know what I feel."

Chip put his hands on his hips. "Maybe not. But whatever it is, you're doing jack shit about it, other than making everyone here miserable with your shitty attitude. Now cowboy up and do something about it." Chip led Daisy out of the barn, and the door banged closed after him. When in the hell did everyone in this family learn how to make a dramatic exit?

Alan stared after Chip and then turned to Maribelle and Centauri, who were both looking back at him. "Do you have an opinion too?"

They headed away. Maribelle went back to eating, and Centauri turned his back. Alan guessed they had expressed their opinion as well. He went back into the tack room and cleaned up another one of Chip's messes. As he was about to leave, the tack room door slowly slid closed, and the old metal mirror on the back caught his reflection. Chip had told him to cowboy up. The term had stung a little, but Alan began to wonder if he was right. Maybe it was time for him to figure out what he wanted and a way to get it.

CHAPTER 11

GEORGE'S FOOTSTEPS echoed off the walls of Blecham Park's main hall. George didn't remember the place being this sterile and cavernous before.

His mother descended the stairs, the click of her heels joining the sounds already bouncing through the space.

"Where are the tapestries?" he asked. They had always hung on the walls, warming the space and making it feel less... empty.

"I had them taken down and stored. I wanted to see the walls, and this is so much grander." She turned her gaze to the coffered ceiling with its painted and frescoed panels. "This way the ceiling can be the focal point."

George sighed. "Have them put back," he told her flatly.

"I like it this way," she pressed.

There had been a battle brewing between them since he'd gotten home. It seemed his mother had come to like being the one openly in charge, and she wanted to keep it that way. He had never realized what awful taste his mother had until now. The entire house had been sanitized, with dozens of important antiques and artworks stored away so the rooms seemed more open. In the morning room, the flowing draperies that had given the room color had been replaced with neutral tones that made the space look like a blend between Edwardian elegance and a dated sixties ranch. "Well, I don't," he told her. "Put them back."

She walked toward the front door as though she hadn't heard him. That had always been one of her tactics when she didn't like something—just ignore it.

"Alistair," George said as he made his way to open the door, "please have the staff rehang the tapestries as well as replace all the artworks she removed. And for God's sake, rip down those morning room curtains and the ones in the library. I'd also like you to make a list of anything else that was changed while I was away."

"Very good, sir," Alistair said.

"You will not," his mother snapped from the doorway.

"And you can deliver those god-awful curtains to the dower house. If my mother likes them so much, she can decorate her new home with them." George knew that would keep her quiet.

"I am not moving in there. I am perfectly comfortable in my rooms here." She lifted her nose in the air. "And if this is some payback for having you brought home from where you were living, in that...." The way she looked down her nose made George's blood boil. "Your brother was content to have me living here."

"But I'm not. This is my home, and I will live here on my own rather than fight with you. It's time you had a place of your own." He smiled. "Or I'll do what Prince Philip did when he needed to get his mother-in-law out of the house. Turn off the heat and make you as uncomfortable as I can." He smiled, and his mother growled.

"I will not argue with you. I have lunch with the Cavanaughs to discuss a charity drive in half an hour, and I won't be late." She left.

George sighed and held his head in his hands as a headache threatened. The entire time he'd been in Wyoming, he hadn't had a single migraine. And being home a week, he'd had two of them. The doctors thought they were stress-related, and now George had proof, because his mother caused nothing but stress. On top of that, he missed Alan. The other day he had been out riding and had seen one of the villagers on horseback. For a second he had spurred his horse forward, thinking it was Alan. The man had been shocked when George had rounded on him. George felt like a complete idiot and had hurriedly excused himself before riding off, missing Alan even more, especially after he'd had another go-around with his mother.

"Sir...," Alistair prompted gently.

"Please have those things replaced when the staff is able. I don't know what she was thinking, but we will be opening the house for tours this season, and it needs to be ready to receive them. If the important pieces are gone, they'll be disappointed."

"Very good," he said softly. "Do you want me to bring you up something for your head?"

"No. Now that the source of my headache is gone, I think I should be all right. But please get those god-awful curtains gone before mother gets back. I never want to see them again, and you should also arrange to have the dowager house opened and cleaned. My mother is moving out, whether she likes it or not." This was a big house for only him, but it wasn't big enough for him and his mother. "I'll be in the small library if anyone needs me." He had plenty of work to do and plans to make on how to get everything that needed to be done accomplished without draining every cent the dukedom had.

George closed the library door and sat in the same workspace his father had used, trying to figure out how to start. He had the things his father had planned as a starting point, but every time he went over it, it didn't make sense. There were plans for the house and for the grounds, and then for the crops and livestock. It all seemed so damned disjointed that it got George's head spinning and he couldn't make any sense of it.

A knock pulled him out of his thoughts, and he set everything aside, relieved for the break.

"Sir, I brought you some lunch, and we have rehung the curtains. Your mother told us to dispose of them, but we hung them up out of sight in one of the servants' hall closets." They all knew as well as George did that his mother would never go into that area of the house.

"Thank you. What about the tapestries?"

"We sent those out for a gentle cleaning after they were taken down. They should be returned soon, and they'll be hung back where they belong. As for the other items, we'll work on those over the next few days." He smiled. "We all feel the way you do. Blecham Park needs to change, but we should keep what works and makes this place special. And we will do what we can to help."

"Thank you." George hugged the man before he realized what he was doing.

"I see your time in America has changed you," Alistair said.

George had to agree. "They helped me be more open about the things I want and what I expect of others. It's important to maintain a distance, but the people here are part of the family, and we are only going to make this work if we all pull together." And going around issuing orders and expecting them to be obeyed the way his mother tended to do wasn't going to get it done.

"If I may say so, I think your time there did you good. You seem happier in your own skin." He cleared his throat. "Even if there's still a sadness." He said no more, and George went into the day room, where lunch had been set out for him. The room had been set to rights and felt as warm and lively as he remembered. Instead of the beige monstrosities, it now boasted its original light floral damask drapes, which gave the room the feeling of bringing the outdoors inside.

George sat down and ate his lunch quietly. He might as well get used to it. He smiled when he received a message from his business manager that his offer for Centauri had been accepted. He wasn't sure if Alan would be angry with him about that, but there was no way he was going to allow them to lose the ranch where they had made him feel so at home. He got all the potential that little colt had, and they got the resources to build a future. It was a win for everyone, even if he didn't get to see it.

"Sir, Viscount Wendel Brown is out front," Alistair said.

George smiled. "Please show him in and see if the kitchen can make up a plate for him." He set down his fork and stood as Wendel strode in with his usual confidence. Wendel's father was an earl, and he would inherit the title and all that went with it eventually.

"I see you're back from your rambles." He came right up to George, and they exchanged a brief hug. Alistair set down a plate, and they sat. "So how were the wilds of the American west?" Wendel was many things, but first and foremost he was a creature of comfort.

"It was amazing." George leaned over the table. "I met a cowboy."

Wendel smirked. "You're kidding. Did he give you a ride on his horse? Or maybe you gave him one." He snickered. George knew he was joking, but he didn't feel like smiling at this kind of reference to Alan. "Oh... I see."

"No, you don't. The people I met were genuine, kind, and hardworking. None of this smiling at a party and then telling stories to the tabloids the following day. They were good people, and Alan was...." He swallowed, because the words just wouldn't come.

Wendel's sculpted eyebrows rose higher. "My, my. I never thought I'd see the day when I'd see any man turn your head. I was starting to wonder if you were going to remain an old bachelor duke your entire life and have your bits fall off or something." He took a bite of the pork and hummed. "Damn, this is good." Sometimes Wendel could give his listeners whiplash.

"We will not talk about my bits. You'll shock Alistair and the others who keep this house running, and I like to keep my staff happy." Wendel was notorious for not being able to keep help, which was why he still lived at home with his parents. Well, that and the savings on rent, which allowed him the money to spend a good amount of his time in the various London clubs populated by men who catered to Wendel's very particular delights.

"Tell, did he give a great ride?" Wendel asked in a stage whisper.

"Stop. Alan wasn't one of your playthings," George scolded.

Wendel set down his fork, eyes widening. "Did you fall in love with this cowboy?" he asked. "You did. I can tell by the look in your eyes. You met some luscious cowboy and had to leave him behind." He clicked his tongue. "Well, I know just the remedy for that. We can travel down to London, and you can get yourself lost in a sea of men who would love to make you forget everything."

George rolled his eyes. "That's a lot more your milieu than mine." The truth was that he wasn't interested in anyone else. He wanted Alan.

"Do you text him?" Wendel asked.

George shrugged.

"What kind of bloody long-distance boyfriend are you if you don't text the bloke or have late-night naked FaceTime sessions?" He took a few more bites. "What did you do, just come back here and think, 'Well, that's the end. I'll be miserable and mope around my huge-arsed estate, wishing he were here, rather than make an effort'?" Wendel emptied his wineglass and poured himself some more.

"You think I should text him?" George asked, his heart suddenly racing.

"Obviously." He leaned back in his chair, sipped more of George's nice white wine, and got settled. "Do you think I'm going to leave so you can call him in person?" He crossed his arms over his chest.

"It's a seven-hour time difference." George did a quick calculation and sent a message. Alan was always up early, so maybe he'd be out in the barn or in the fields seeing to the herd. George could almost see him, either with the horses or riding one of those snow machines, loaded down with feed and sliding over the snow. Though what he saw most often when he closed his eyes was Alan laid out on the bed, his bare backside on the sheets so George could run his hands down his back and over the curve of that perfect cowboy arse, then down his thick, corded legs that would twitch under his touch.

His phone vibrated, and George smiled at the reply.

"What did he say? Something wicked?" Wendel grabbed the phone. "Hey."

"Awww, he says he's angry with you because you went behind his back and bought the colt. Then he sends a tongue-sticking-out smiley face." George snatched his phone back. "What does that mean? *You* bought a horse?"

"Yes, I did. Dad and Mark had polo ponies, but I don't give a nut about polo. It's boring and pretentious. I'm arranging to sell the ones that are still here. A number of Mark's buddies are interested in them. I'm going to shift the stables to training racers, and this colt is going to be where I start. You should see him. The most beautiful little colt, with a great lineage. What I need to do is find someone to do the training."

"What about the existing trainer?"

"He's going to work for Sir Harold Miller in a few months once all the sales are completed. I took care of him." George was determined to look after all of the people he might shift out of a position because of the changes he thought needed to be made. "My next task in that area is to look for a trainer I can trust." He originally thought about doing it himself, but he would need someone more permanent as he grew his program.

"So you've figured out what you want to do with the stables, and the house…?"

George sighed. "I'm undoing the ghastly things my mother did and moving her to the dower house. You'll probably hear the screaming all the way to London when it sinks in, but I'm not going to live with my mother."

Wendel lifted his glass. "That's one decision I agree with." Wendel and his mother hated each other with a passion. "She seems to have done a good job managing the estate while you were gone."

"And she brought me home because I had to sign some things, but then she wanted to go on running things her way and let me stand to the side."

Wendel shrugged. "You were never much interested in the place anyway. You wanted to run with your animals and look after everyone else's. You could still do that if you just let your mother do what she wants." He shivered. "Did I just say that?" Those were words George never expected to hear either.

"It seems if I did that, by the time she was done, the place would look like a tomb and all the tourists would be disappointed as all hell." George stood and wandered the room. "What I really need to do is figure out a way for the house to pay for itself. I've thought of opening it at times for banquets and dinners and such, but the wear and tear on the place might get to be more than it's worth." George just hadn't come up with an idea that would tie everything together, and it was driving him crazy. He knew he'd eventually hit on it. "I want something unique. Plenty of these places have been turned into hotels or places for fancy dos. I want this to be one of a kind." He opened the door and stepped out onto the terrace, with Wendel following, carrying his glass.

"The grounds...." Wendel sighed.

"I know. They were lovely when granddad had the place, but my father didn't care for them, so he just added to the lawns and planted some trees, most of which makes no sense." There was so much to do, and George had no idea where to even start. "I know I don't want fussy, but a proper country landscape would be preferable to the jumble of today." His phone vibrated again, and he smiled and answered Alan's text, snapped a few pictures of the area around him, and sent them back.

"What did he say?" Wendel asked, leaning against the balustrade.

For a second, George wondered why he and Wendel had never been any more than friends, but then he chuckled to himself. He knew what real passion was now. Wendel knew his way around a man's body, George was pretty sure. But he couldn't see him making George forget his own name and half the world around him with just a touch. And while Wendel dressed well, he didn't hold a candle to his cowboy in a pair of tight jeans.

George shook his head as his phone vibrated again. Did he have the right to think of Alan as his when he was thousands of miles away, trying and failing to move on?

George grinned. "He told me it looks like sheep and cattle country." Alan was right, of course. The estate had thousands of sheep and a few hundred head of Jerseys. George also had the income from a number of other land holdings, as well as that from trusts set up by his grandfather and great-grandfather. He began typing an answer as a picture came through. It was Daisy and her pups playing. He sighed and wished he could be there. Then another picture of Centauri followed.

"What is that expression for?" Wendel came closer. "Did he send you sexy pics?" Wendel rolled his eyes and laughed. "I see—dogs and horses."

"The dogs I rescued in a blizzard, and that's the horse that I bought." He was still looking at the picture of the little colt when his phone buzzed again. *I took this one for you special.*

George nearly dropped the phone when a photo of Alan flashed on his screen. He was shirtless and still wet from the shower. The expression was pure Alan, and George's throat tightened. When Wendel tried to peek, he pulled the phone away.

That's some view. Best one in Wyoming. He sent it quickly and then slipped his phone into his pocket, away from prying eyes.

"You really do have it bad for this guy." Wendel turned to go back inside. "You know, there's only one way to get over something like that. Find yourself a new man."

George followed and closed the door against the chill. "Or get the old one back." He wished he knew how to make that happen.

GEORGE MANAGED to avoid his mother until lunch the following day.

"I won't have it," she snapped as she strode into the room, glaring at him. "You have them undoing everything I did. I know you want this place to look like a throwback to an eighties horror movie, but I don't."

"Mother." He sighed. "You seem to think that because Mark and father are gone, you rule the roost now. Father let you bully him sometimes, but you won't do that to me. I went away to try to figure some things out, and I expected you to manage things here and further Father's plans. Instead, you came up with ones of your own, ones that I don't agree with. Thankfully Alistair and the staff had the foresight to pack away what you decided didn't fit your style. What were your plans?" He set down his fork and glared at her across the morning room table. "I got a call from an auction house in London, and I canceled the contract you signed. They may try to put up a fuss, but I explained that you didn't have the authority and you didn't own the items in question. Whether they decide to take action against you is their choice." He returned to his lunch with a small smile.

She blanched. "I intended to pay for the roof," she said as she sat down. Alistair brought her a plate and then left the room.

"Well, I don't intend to sell the family treasures to try to pay for it." He was still working out how that was going to happen. "Regardless, I have left instructions for the staff to return things where they belong.

And I plan to inventory everything in the attics and storage rooms—first to see what treasures are up there, and second, maybe we can sell some of that and have a good old-fashioned clear out. Your auction house was more than willing to help in that regard." George couldn't help smiling, because it had worked out well in the end.

"Well, I suppose that's something," she said overdramatically, and slowly began eating the salmon with orange sauce. "You know that there are expectations beyond just managing the estate. You are going to have to find a wife, marry, and carry on the line." She was changing the subject. "I've met a number of charming ladies, and—"

George put his hand up. "Stop and pull yourself out of your dream world. I'm gay, and you know it. So just stop." He stood and glared at her. "How many times do I have to tell you that I won't marry someone like that? I am not interested in women that way. When the time comes, I'll find a surrogate and have a child in my own way." He placed his hands on the table. "Mother, the dower house is calling you."

She stood and glared back at him. "I told you already I am not moving there."

"Then figure out where else you are going to live, because I'm not going to fight with you every day about everything. I went to America because I needed to feel free for a while. The mantle of expectations was more than I had ever asked for. But I see now that what I was doing was putting off the inevitable... and dealing with you." He calmed himself, because he was on the verge of saying things that he couldn't take back. "I don't want to live my life the way you seem to think I should. And that's fine. You are entitled to your opinion. However, I don't want to listen to it day in and day out. Therefore, you need to find yourself a place of your own. The dower house is there, and we will work to clean it. You will have a place of your own, and you can bland it up all you like. Father saw to it that you have an income, so you will need to live within your means." He was pretty proud that he kept his temper in check. "Unless you wish to secure a home of your own. That is also up to you."

She sighed. "I could move into the London place," she offered.

"No, Mother. You can live in the dower house or find a place of your own." He was getting tired of going round and round about this. It wasn't like the dower house was a wreck. It was eight rooms and just needed some cleaning and freshening up. No, the real reason was that his mother loved being in control, and George wasn't going to fight her every day for everything he had to do. Doing what he needed to do in order to ensure the estate's future was going to be hard, and doing it alone, nearly impossible. But trying to accomplish what he needed to with someone fighting him was bordering on the miraculous.

She said nothing and simply stared at him the way she had when he was a child. It wasn't going to work, but still....

He sat down and returned to his lunch. "You can sit there all you want, but my mind is made up. Now, can we stop fighting about this and talk about something else?" His head pounded, but he was not going to let her see how she got to him.

"What happened to you?" she asked.

George smiled. "You mean what happened to the person who just let you do whatever you want? He went to America and found himself. He found someone to love and who loved him back. That's what happened." He took a bite and swallowed it. "I figured some things out while I was there." He held her gaze. "I was running away because I didn't want any of this. I wanted it all to just go away and for Mark and Father to not have died. That way I could have my life back. But I can't have any of those things, no matter how much I might wish for them." All he could think of was what Alan would have done. When his father died, he'd stayed and taken over the ranch. He'd stepped up and done what was necessary. "I learned that I needed to cowboy up and do what I had to, and if I'm going to do that, then I'll do things my way and with everything I have." Because that was what Alan would do. "And that's what I'm doing. I am slowly developing a vision for this place. One that will move us into the future and make the most of our past. I haven't figured it out yet, but I will." He took a final bite, swallowed, and placed his napkin on the table. "I have work to do. I suggest you start packing your things." It was time to take charge. He had put off doing his duty and taking up the reins for too long. He just wished he didn't have to do it alone.

CHAPTER 12

ALAN WAS not going to get used driving on the other side of the road. Just riding in the car drove him crazy. He finally sat back and hoped to hell the woman behind the wheel knew what she was doing.

"Have you been to England before?" she asked in a heavy accent that Alan had to concentrate on to understand.

"I've never been anywhere before." He looked out the windows at the landscape shrouded in low clouds. The wet green grasses against bare trees gave the scene a closed-in feel, like it was waiting for something to happen. And maybe it was. Spring should be around the corner, but it hadn't reached this far north quite yet. "This looks a lot like home once the snow is gone and the grass starts growing. The trees just haven't started to leaf out."

"That will be a while yet," she said and checked her phone. "I have to ask. Do you really want me to take you to Blecham Park?"

"Don't you know where it is?" Alan asked. George had given the address to his mother, and she had eventually shown Alan the note and given him the details once he had decided he had to see George again and try to figure things out. The weeks they'd been apart, Alan had only been going through the motions, and his mother had finally told him to "shit or get off the pot." She said she could manage the ranch and that it was his time to manage his own life. So here he was on his way to George's, hoping they didn't slam the door in his face.

"Of course I do," the woman, a year or two older than him, said. "But are you sure His Grace will see you?" She pulled to a stop and turned around to look him over again. "He's a very busy man, and people just don't go up to Blecham Park and say, 'Hey, knock, knock, let me in, I want to say hello to the duke.'" She acted a little like he was crazy. "I could just take you to a nice little inn where you could have a look around the area."

Alan swallowed hard, holding his phone, tempted to message George and tell him where he was and what his plans were. But he was afraid that George might tell him not to come, and Alan needed to see him. Maybe he was totally stupid to fly all this way, but if George did turn him away, Alan would do as she suggested, find an inn, see a little of the sights, and then go home to the ranch to go on with his life. "I should be fine. Just take me to this Blecham Park."

"Okay," she agreed and continued on. A moment later she turned off the main road onto a drive and then up to a gate, which was open. She continued through, and Alan gasped as what he would describe as a palace came into view. The place was huge, with a front that seemed to shine even on this cloudy day. The main building with huge columns in front extended to wings on either side in the same stone. A portico dominated the front of the building, and a stone area extended from the front, bordered by a stone wall topped with wrought iron. Large lampposts indicated the front entrance. The driver pulled to a stop outside that formal entrance. "Do you want me to wait?"

Alan peered up to the top of the front of the building and opened the door. He picked up his hat off the seat next to him and plopped it on his head. "If you wouldn't mind." Jesus, all he could think was that he had come all this way, and maybe George wasn't home, or maybe he'd changed his mind and figured out Alan wasn't worth all this trouble.

Stone crunched under his boots as he pulled his coat around him against the cold wind and made his way to the front door. He knocked with his knuckles and then stepped back to look up at the stone coffered ceiling above him. No one answered, and he looked back at the car before using the huge knocker.

The impressively heavy door swung inward. "Can I help you?" Alistair asked and then smiled. "Mr. Justice," he said happily. "I didn't know you were arriving. His Grace isn't at home."

Alan nodded. "I see. Well, would you please tell him that I stopped by and...." He wasn't sure what to do now, if George was gone.

"He's expected home in an hour or so. Please come in." He motioned, and a man about Alan's age in black pants and a white shirt, wearing some sort of apron, hurried by. "Stewart will get your bags."

"I need to pay my driver. She was nice enough to bring me from the train station." He suppressed a yawn. The flight to London had been long enough, but it had taken hours on a train to get this far north. Alan pulled out his wallet, but Alistair shook his head and had a quiet conversation with Stewart, who took care of things with the driver after getting Alan's bags. Then he sent her on her way.

"This is a real surprise, and I know His Grace will be pleased to see you." He motioned inside, and Alan took two steps and seemed to enter another world. Acres of marble and stone, walls covered with scenes of animals, riders on horseback, and prey. It took his breath away.

Ladies and men hurried past the top of the stairs and then returned, carrying suitcases, trunks, and boxes. "Someone moving?" Alan asked. "Do they need help?" He was already pushing up his sleeves.

"The dowager duchess is moving out at the moment. The house is in a state of near chaos, which is why His Grace left. If you'll follow me into the small library, I can have some tea brought in and you may get comfortable until His Grace arrives." Alistair seemed pleased to see him.

"I don't want to put anyone out," he said gently, unsure where to look. There was just so much to see. He followed Alistair into an opulent room lined with bookshelves and bookcases with glass-front doors. "You said this is the small library?" Alan swallowed hard.

"Yes. It's His Grace's office and sitting room. Would you like to see the big library?" Alistair opened another door, and Alan peered into a room at least twice the size of the one he was in.

"Suffering cats. How does anyone find anything?" he asked. Two walls of the room, which had to be twenty feet high, were lined with books. As he stepped in and turned around, he saw that two huge paintings flanked the door he'd come in, with smaller works above them and over the door. The other wall was mostly windows, with the curtains currently drawn. "My God. I thought places like this only existed in fairy tales or on television." He stepped back into the other room, and Alistair closed the door.

"I'll see to your tea." Alistair left before Alan could explain that he didn't drink tea. Then he shrugged and sat in one of the chairs. He sighed and stretched his legs out, sinking into the upholstery like it had been made for him.

A tall clock ticked softly, and he let himself just breathe and try to relax. He was so tired, and he'd traveled such a long away. All he could think about was seeing George again and maybe resting his eyes for a few minutes.

GEORGE ARRIVED home to less chaos than when he'd left. Many of his mother's things had been taken over to the dower house already, but the staff was still bustling with what George hoped was the last of it. At least his mother was nowhere to be seen, so that was a win. Before he'd left, she had decided that today was the day she'd vent her displeasure at him… again. George had made up his mind, and his mother's behavior had only reinforced that he'd made the right decision.

"Is that the last of it?" George asked Stewart, who had come down the stairs to meet him.

"Yes, my lord," he stammered. "We are nearly done, and I believe her ladyship is over at the dower house now, overseeing the setup."

George had a number of questions about who exactly his mother was overseeing.

"Where is Alistair?" he asked just as the man himself came in with a tray. "Thank you, Stewart. I appreciate your help in getting her things moved." He smiled and made a note to make sure that anyone involved with his mother's move got a bonus. At least his head had stopped pounding.

George inhaled. "Coffee, Alistair?" he asked. It was about time for tea, and he had been looking forward to something hot. But he never had coffee after breakfast, as Alistair was well aware. "What's the occasion? Something to fortify all of us after my mother's dramatic departure?"

"Well, yes and no, sir. You have a guest. I put him in the small library until you returned. I thought this particular guest would prefer coffee." Something in Alistair's tone caught George off guard. Maybe it was the slight smile, but that could be attributable to the fact that his mother was leaving, taking her brand of chaos along with her. Alistair loved order, planning, and knowing what was to come. His mother was none of those things.

George motioned for Alistair to go first. Otherwise the man would stand there waiting for George all day. George knew he was just doing his job, but he didn't want his home to feel like he was living in a rerun of *Downton Abbey*. He held the door, and Alistair went inside. George followed and stopped as soon as the familiar boots and long legs spread out across the plush rug came into view. Alan sat in his chair, hat tipped forward over his eyes, hands in his lap, chest slowly rising and falling, those damned long legs encased in jeans too sinfully tight to be legal. It all took his breath away.

"When did he get here?" George asked Alistair very quietly so he didn't disturb Alan.

"Maybe an hour ago. My guess is that he's been up since leaving Wyoming and he didn't stop to rest in London." Alistair smiled. "I believe he was very anxious to see you." He turned and left the room, closing the door behind him without a sound.

Quietly, George poured himself some of the coffee and took a few biscuits before settling in one of the other chairs. He sipped and munched without making a sound, just watching Alan sleep.

He could hardly believe he was here. If he wasn't seeing Alan with his own eyes.... Alan had come all this way to see him. They had texted every day since the day of his lunch with Wendel. Even yesterday, Alan had sent a few texts that George now realized were from airports and places where he'd had cell service. The man had kept his upcoming visit a surprise, and it was one heck of a doozy.

"George...," Alan said as he slid his eyes open. "I'm sorry. I didn't mean to fall asleep." He jumped to his feet, looking strange in this room in his jeans and flannel shirt, and yet to George's eyes, he looked completely at home.

George set his cup on the table and went over to Alan. "I'm glad you're here." He grinned and grabbed Alan by the belt, pulling him right to him. Sliding an arm around his neck, he tugged Alan forward, bringing their lips together. The kiss nearly buckled his knees, and Alan hugged him tightly, keeping him upright as he took George's lips in a fierce kiss that raised the temperature in the room by a dozen degrees in as many seconds.

"Okay. So coming here wasn't a bad idea," Alan whispered.

"God, no. But why *are* you here? Has something happened?" he asked.

Alan nodded. "My mother pushed me to no end and told me that if I didn't stop moping around the house all the damned time, she was going to kick my cowboy butt all the way to Cheyenne and throw me on a damned plane herself."

George chuckled. He could hear Maureen in those words.

"She told me that it was time she took over the ranch and took charge of her life. After Dad died, I think she retreated, and I just stepped up and took on the ranch because I had to. But Mom said it was time I lived my own life."

George understood that. It was the same for him. It had been Alan and his family who had helped him realize that he needed to stop running away and cowboy up. "Maybe we were both running away."

Alan nodded. "I didn't realize I was until I poked my head up and knew that I'd buried a lot of myself in the ranch. It was easier than going out in the world and making my own way." He pulled George to him once again. "I'm not running anymore. I came here to try to figure some things out." He backed away, and George watched as he gazed over the room. "Is this where you grew up? I'd be afraid to do anything in these rooms in case I broke something." Alan grinned. "But could you imagine roller skating in here?"

George laughed. "We were never allowed down here until we were older. Mark and I had a nursery and playroom on the second floor, and that's where our toys stayed. We spent some time with our parents each day, but mostly we had nannies until we went away to school." George's childhood wasn't bad, but it hadn't been an emotionally warm one as far as his parents were concerned.

Alan stepped back. "You know I'm just a roughneck cowboy, and this is…." He swallowed hard and pulled back farther. "Maybe this wasn't such a good idea."

"What, coming here?" George closed the distance between them once more. "I think it was the best idea you've ever had. And as for all this, it's part of what I have to deal with. The house is more of a museum than a home. It's filled with art and sculptures that members of my family have collected over a number of centuries."

"But I don't belong here," Alan whispered. "My boots will track mud in on the carpets, and…." George went to the tray and poured Alan a cup of coffee. "See, these are so dainty. What if I break one?"

George laughed. "Those cups, while dainty-looking, cost like a pound each at one of the local shops. I don't use the good stuff unless I'm having company. Trust me, what you see here is for show. I use this room as an office because it's warm and quiet. It's also where my father worked, as well as my grandfather, so I feel a connection to them here." He waited while Alan finished his coffee and had something to eat. "Do you want the ten-pound tour?" he asked, taking Alan's hand. "Or I could show you upstairs. I'm sure Alistair already had your things moved to one of the guest rooms."

"One of them?"

"Yeah. I think there are about eight or so." He took Alan's hand and led him through the large library, the morning room, dining room, and the ladies' sitting room, as well as the great hall, hoping he didn't overwhelm Alan too much with all the opulence that surrounded them. "All of this is just part of the estate. In a few months, this part of the house will be open to tourists. Because of its location, the morning room is not part of the tour. It and the small library are the two rooms I use all year. The rest of the main floor is on the tour, as is this." George opened the door off the north side of the hall.

Alan stepped in and paused, his mouth open. "Is this a ballroom?"

"Yes." George couldn't help lifting his gaze upward to the huge chandeliers that hung from the frescoed ceiling. "The tour guides can tell you who painted the ceiling, but I just love this room."

Alan's footsteps echoed off the polished and intricately inlaid wood floor. "You could hold one heck of a dance in here." He turned full circle. "Is that for the band?"

George nodded. "It's a grand space, but one that doesn't get used all that much any longer. My mother used to have a holiday party in here and a few other gatherings, but I don't foresee using it much. I've toyed with allowing the space to be let for weddings and things, but then there's the issue of the food and people in the rest of the house."

Alan just seemed to be taking it all in, and George grew quiet. He still hadn't figured out what he was going to do, but he wanted more than to have the place open for tours. Maybe using this room for events, with certain rules, wasn't such a bad idea. One thing George was sure of: he didn't want to become a caterer. That was out of the question. Those facilities and capabilities were too specialized.

"Then find someone you can work with to do the food," Alan offered as he turned slowly. "You don't have to do it all. Find good people you can partner with. It's what we do on the ranch. Our operation isn't big enough to have all its own equipment, but I use Vasquez's hay cutter and his baler. When it's time to cut, I'm always there to lend a hand and my truck to pull the wagons, as are a number of other ranchers. Then, when it's time, we use the equipment as well, and we all do our share of the upkeep and maintenance. We've all kept that equipment running for a decade or more past its lifespan." He moved toward the door. "Like on a ranch, you gotta make hay with everything you got." Alan whistled. "And this is a lot."

"Yeah," George agreed. "I just haven't figured what I can do to tie everything together." He followed and closed the door to keep the heat in the rest of the house. That room was maintained, but it was only heated to a certain point. "Come on. I'll take you up and show you your room. You probably will want to lie down and try to rest for a while. Flying can really take it out of you."

Alan followed him along the main upstairs hallway. "Are all these people in the paintings related to you?"

"Yes. A lot of these houses have a portrait gallery, and my family put them here. It's kind of strange, because usually they're on the floor below so they can be shown off to others. At one point those rooms were filled with other collected artworks, so the portraits got moved up here. There are a lot of them."

"Is there one of you?" Alan asked.

"Not yet. I will have to have one commissioned at some point. That is my father, the tenth duke, and there's my grandfather. They look so serious." George came to a stop beside Alan, taking his hand. "My father was a serious man, but he wasn't harsh or mean. Sometimes I think the estate took more out of him than he let on. There's so much to juggle to keep everything running right."

"In ranching, we all find our strengths. No one ranch can do it all. Not without having a huge operation, and even those guys don't do that. They often have a main business and then one or two side gigs. We run the cattle—that's what pays the bills. But Chip loves horses, and so does Mama, so we have those too. Some we use for riding, and others we breed because we get good foals. So what is it that makes Blecham Park special?"

"We raise amazing sheep with high-quality wool, and we raise some beef because we needed to diversify so we didn't have everything in one basket," George explained as Alistair came down the hall. He opened the door to the blue room.

"I put Mr. Justice in here for his stay," he said. "You've been unpacked, and if there's anything you need, please let us know." He seemed excited. Well, as close as Alistair ever came to that.

"Thank you," Alan said, and Alistair left the room.

"I'll leave you to rest for a while." George had plenty of work he should try to do.

"You don't have to go unless you want to." Alan sat on the side of the bed and took off his boots before stretching out his long legs. Those eyes drew George in, and he slowly approached. Alan reached up and drew him down, kissing him deeply. "I know I'm too tired for anything athletic, but I've been dreaming of this for weeks."

George kicked off his shoes and then pulled the curtains closed while Alan lay on the bed. George climbed in after him and pulled the duvet up over both of them. They were still dressed, but George didn't care. Everything fell into place as he held Alan in the darkness. Weeks of restless sleep caught up to him, with George breathing deeply, pressed to Alan's back.

"I missed you," Alan said softly into the darkened room. "I was short with everyone and just… unhappy."

"Me too. I think that's why Alistair is doing his version of a happy dance." He chuckled. Alistair would never put on any sort of display, but his near smile and light demeanor spoke volumes.

"Is he really your friend? Because if so, why make him a butler?" Alan asked as he rolled over.

"Because it's what he does. Alistair could run a hotel in London if he wanted. He's trained, and he has major skills." George stroked his hand down Alan's rough cheek.

"Then why not put him to work?" Alan yawned and closed his eyes. "I think I can really sleep for the first time since you left." He sighed.

"Good. Just relax, and we'll talk later. Maybe you and I can look at the rest of the operations here on the estate."

"Looking forward to it," Alan whispered as he tugged George close, and very soon, Alan's breathing evened out, and George knew he was asleep.

George wasn't tired, but he didn't want to leave Alan either. He felt like pinching himself just to make sure he wasn't dreaming. But Alan was too warm and his soft snoring so reminiscent of their nights in Wyoming that George let himself relax as well, and soon he dozed off too.

GEORGE WOKE and carefully slipped out of bed. Alan was still sound asleep, and George watched him for a few minutes, then left the room, taking his shoes with him. He found Alistair in the morning room, setting things up for dinner. George loved this room even after dark, and it was more casual than the dining room. With only him and now Alan in the house, it was a more comfortable place for them to have dinner.

"Alan is still asleep."

Alistair finished what he was doing. "If I may say so, you might want to wake him. Otherwise he won't sleep at all tonight." He said no more, but the inference that George might want him awake definitely hung in the air. George rolled his eyes and returned to the room, where Alan lay curled up in the bedding like some kind of sausage in pastry. He sat on the edge of the bed, gently rocking Alan's shoulder.

"What time is it?"

"Supper will be ready soon," George said softly as Alan slid his eyes open.

"I was dreaming that I was here with you, and then I half woke up and went back to sleep because I knew it couldn't be true. Yet here you are," Alan said, yawning as he sat up. "How late is it?" He turned toward the window curtains, which only showed black around them.

"A little after six in the evening," George told him. "Supper will be in the morning room. Yeah, I know, but I like it in there, and the dining room is so formal and stuffy. If you want to clean up, the bathroom is through that door. My room is through the door right there, and the dressing room is between them. That's where your clothes have been hung up and laid out."

Alan wiped his hands down his face. "I'm so in over my head. Do I need to dress up or something?" He seemed on edge suddenly.

"No, you don't." He leaned over and kissed Alan lightly. "You just come down the way you'd normally dress for dinner. We're not having a party or something. It will be just you and me." He patted Alan on the shoulder. "Please don't worry about all the finery and stuff. This is just a house, nothing more, and I want you to be comfortable here."

"But it's huge."

"Yes. It's a big place, and I need some help to care for it." He stayed sitting and took a deep breath. "Back in Wyoming, I fell in love with you for who you were, and you seemed to do the same with me. I am that person you knew in Wyoming." He waved his hands toward the window. "People out there are going to bow and scrape and have many different titles for me. Your Grace, my lord, Duke… each of them a title that goes with the position I hold. You call me George because that's the man I am and the person I always want to be."

"How can I fit in with all of this?" Alan asked quietly.

"Just be yourself. Don't fit in. Be the man you are and stand out. That's why I love you. Alan Justice is always true to who he is and the man inside. And I'll tell you this: if someone doesn't like you, they can go jump in the lake." George pointed. "There's one just off to the side, so they don't have to leave the property." He couldn't stop himself from making the joke, and thankfully Alan chuckled.

MORNING CAME way too early. Alan snored softly next to him, his warm skin pressed to George's. Now this was something he could get used to for the rest of his life.

Over dinner last night they had talked about everything, and Alan had brought him up to date. Centauri was growing well, and both mother and colt were doing fine. Apparently the little one was very inquisitive. Daisy was settling in. Chip had found homes for two of the puppies, but he and Maureen had each claimed one of the other two, so they all had good homes. Chip was busy making his plans for school in the fall.

"I'll be happy to send him a recommendation on my stationery." That would get admissions departments' attention. Maureen was stepping in to run the ranch.

"Mom worked with my father all those years, and I think she needed some time in order to step back into it again," Alan had said with dark eyes. "But that leaves me out in the cold, in a way." He had sighed as he stared out the windows. "Mom and I developed a plan together before I left, and I think she's happy." He had flashed a strained smile before returning to his dinner of roast lamb from the estate.

George knew in his heart that was Maureen's way of telling Alan that he had his own life to lead and to go out and find it. He would love to see her again… and soon. It wasn't like George could ask his own mother about the questions he had.

George wanted Alan to stay—he really did. But he knew he couldn't just ask him. That would be too easy, and Alan would say no. Alan was a man of action, and he would need something to do.

He pulled on a robe and sat in his chair near the window, looking out over the grounds. The sun was just peeking out, playing tag with the clouds as their shadows rolled across the landscape.

"What time is it?" Alan asked before yawning.

"It's about eight in the morning. I can have breakfast brought up if you like, or we can go down to the morning room." He stood and went over to the bed, where he leaned over Alan. "Damn, I can't tell you how good you look like that."

"What? Jet-lagged and unable to keep my eyes open?" Alan groaned.

"No. Naked and lying in my bed." He breathed deeply. "I kept wondering if this fantasy of mine could possibly come true, and here you are. Not only are you here, but...." He took Alan's lips. Alan wound his arms around him and tugged George back into bed, holding him tightly as he plundered George's lips.

A knock stilled both of them, and George growled softly before backing away.

"Sir... your mother is downstairs in the morning room."

He sighed. "I had better go on down and see what she wants." He stood, looking at the amazing figure Alan cut. On a horse or in bed, the man was stunning, and George wanted to keep him all to himself. "You can rest if you want or get dressed and come down with me." That was a test of bravery if George had ever seen one. He honestly didn't know what Alan would do, but he got out of bed and went through to the dressing room. George did the same and pulled on clothes for riding. Alan picked up on the theme and pulled on one of his nearly sinful pairs of jeans and a flannel shirt. He also put on his boots and grabbed his hat before following George downstairs to the morning room.

Alistair already had breakfast laid out, and George's mother unexpectedly sat at the table already eating her breakfast. "Good morning, Mother," George said formally. Surprise showed in her eyes as Alan entered the room. "This is Alan Justice."

She narrowed her gaze. "We eat breakfast with the grooms now?" she asked spitefully.

George straightened up. "Alan and his family were kind to me in Wyoming, and Alan is a special guest here." He glared at her. "And you seem to have forgotten your manners and where you live." He used the exact same tone she had used on him whenever he'd put his elbows on the table.

"Good morning, ma'am," Alan said as though George's mother hadn't been rude. Alistair guided Alan through getting his food while George seethed at his mother. She seemed to ignore it and daintily continued eating.

"How long are you staying, Mr. Justice?" she asked in a light tone.

"As long as Alan wants," George answered. "After breakfast, he and I are going out for a ride. I want to show him the estate and explain some of my plans for it. I'm hoping Alan will have some insights for us."

"I'm sure an American cowboy will be an interesting resource," she commented.

George knew she was being catty, but he didn't want to draw additional attention to it. He sighed as Alistair handed him a plate. As he took his food, he changed his mind. "You know, if you can't be civil, then I think you should take breakfast at home," he said gently, knowing that would get her goat. It seemed with her, it was going to be a game of one-upmanship until she realized she wasn't going to cow him. "Alan has been running his family ranch since his father passed away. He has a great deal of experience with agribusiness, and that's the primary purpose of the estate. We raise sheep and some cattle. I want to make sure we're getting the most from our resources." He took a chair next to Alan. "And as we transition away from horses for polo, I want to shift to raising horses for racing. We have the training area already, and I have no intention of taking up polo."

"Your father would roll over in his grave," she said snidely.

"Can I ask why, ma'am? Would he want George to raise animals that he has no use for?" Alan asked. "He told me his father and brother loved the sport, but he doesn't. It seems like a waste of resources to keep them. It makes more sense to raise horses for something he enjoys." He took a few bites and smiled. "Alistair, this is amazing, though I don't get the beans, but everything else is so good."

"I'll be sure to let the cook know," Alistair said without breaking a smile, the amusement in his eyes not going unnoticed.

"Thank you," Alan added with better manners than George's mother. He continued to eat like he was starving, and his mother turned up her nose, setting her fork aside.

"I believe I've had enough." She stood, and George did as well. Alan looked at them both in amusement and followed suit until she left the room.

"I'm sorry about her behavior. Most people are much more... gracious than she is." George remembered something. "I'll be right back." He hurried to his office and returned with a folded paper. "This is a map of the estate lands and what they are being used for currently."

He set it on the table. "As you can see, there is plenty of sheep grazing, and some is set aside as wild heath. That's mostly used for hunting and such—pheasant, grouse, that sort of thing. I want to keep it wild and leave it to nature. This is the area where we graze cattle."

Alan nodded. "What's that?"

"The visitor center. It's where tourists buy the tickets to tour the house. There's a small gift shop where we have a few things about the house."

"Do you sell your lamb there? How about your beef?" Alan asked, and George shrugged. "Why not? You eat it. Our ranch survived because we grew a lot of what we ate and raised good-quality beef. But we get wholesale prices. If you sold your meat and your wool, things like that, in your own shop, you would get full retail." Alan leaned closer and pointed at the map. "What is this used for?"

"One of the locals raises bees. That part of the property is a wildflower meadow, and he keeps his bees there."

"Sell his honey in the gift shop as well," Alan offered. "What else are you producing?"

They ate and talked about the estate, as well as some of George's plans, ideas, and hopes. He told him about the attic auction idea, as well as some others running around in his head. It all came spilling out, and Alan listened, taking it all in. "Can we go out for a ride so I can see all this?"

"Parts of the estate we can see via rover, and others on horseback. Why don't we start with those parts first?" George guided Alan out back. He made sure they had on the right gear before leading him out to the stables.

"These are some fine horses," Alan said as he greeted each of them. "What babies."

"They are. But these are being sold, because the last thing I need is a string of polo ponies when I don't play polo." George smiled. "This is our trainer, Glenn Winsome." Glenn approached, looking dour, taking off his hat as he neared. "Glenn?" George asked.

"I'm sorry to bother you with me troubles, Your Grace, but Sir Harold has fallen and broken his leg. It's very bad, and the doctors have said that he won't be able to ride and...." He swallowed, his cheeks pinking.

"I'm sorry to hear that. I take it he has no need for a trainer for his string," George said, clueing in to the problem. "Glenn, this is Alan Justice from Wyoming." They shook hands.

"You keep the animals in fine condition," Alan said. "Very well cared for." He patted the nose of the nearest animal, and Glenn smiled.

"They're like my babies," Glenn said. "I've been training here on the estate since I was a lad."

"Then why are you leaving, if I may ask?" Alan seemed so genuine.

"His Grace doesn't need a trainer if he's selling the ponies, and I'm getting up in years. Sir Harold was in need of a trainer, and shifting over to him would be easy because I've known his horses and operation almost as long as I've been part of the one here."

Alan turned to him, his gaze not missing much. "Have you trained horses for jumping or flat racing, like George is looking into?"

"Yes, sir."

"It would be a shame to let go of the kind of knowledge you have." Alan's face lit up. "Back home, I've seen ranchers fail even though they had money and lots of land... but they didn't understand their animals or the land they were on. You know both." He nodded and said no more.

Glenn hurried away and had his grandson, the stable lad, saddle horses for them.

"I don't have a western saddle like you're used to," Glenn told Alan, who nodded.

"I suspect I'll get used to it," Alan told him and mounted his horse like he was born there. Damn, he was fine, and desire washed over George.

George mounted and led them off to the more remote parts of the property.

"Can I ask why you don't just keep Glenn on? I know racing is pretty specialized, but...."

"Have you done it?" George asked lightly.

Alan shrugged. "No. But I probably could. I used to race a lot, and if you keep Glenn on, you'll have someone dedicated to your horse program. You could probably find someone to help with the things Glenn doesn't know. Knowledge like Glenn's can't be easily replaced."

"Is that what you'd do?"

Alan chuckled. "If it were up to me, I wouldn't do the racing thing at all. Keep horses here for riding and breed good stock. Maybe horses to help work the sheep. Ones that will benefit the estate. I'm sure Glenn would love to do that. Raise and breed horses to sell—even use the stables as a revenue stream and board horses there. Glenn could manage all that in his sleep, I'm sure." Alan pulled to a stop.

"Is something wrong?" George asked.

"Just that I missed the real point." His eyes gleamed. "You don't need to do anything. When you sell your horses, where will they go?" Alan asked.

"To other trainers and…." George shook his head. "God's balls," he said, just like his father. "We keep the stable as a polo training ground. Let others board their horses here. Glenn is well respected."

"Exactly. You don't just let go of the polo ponies you have. Offer to board and have Glenn train them. Bring in others as well, and you have a thriving business around what you and your people already do well. Glenn keeps his job and his home, and you have an asset that no one else has."

Alan started forward once again, and this time George had to keep up, both with him and with the way his mind worked. Could the answer be that simple?

"But what about Centauri?"

"Bring him here, let Glenn work with him, then see what he turns out to be. Meanwhile, you can transform your stables into a revenue source." Alan stopped. "That was one of the things that my father did wrong. He didn't diversify the ranch, and you saw the mess we were in." He reined his horse to a gentle stop. "If it wasn't for you and for Centauri…. Well, you have the chance to rectify that." Alan started forward again, and George figured clearing the air would be good. He urged his horse on, with Alan right behind them, the crisp air blowing the cobwebs out of his mind.

"What is this?" Alan asked after they slowed.

"One of the sheep meadows." George pointed toward where part of the flock grazed over the green, flowing land. "We produce a huge amount of wool each year." He anticipated Alan's question. "We sell almost all of it."

"Is there a place that will spin and dye it for you? Even a small portion of it."

George had already added that to his mental list. "I bet there is." His head spun. "We could sell it in the shop here and maybe at a few places in town."

Alan grinned. "Now you're thinking like a prosperous businessman." They continued on, returning to the stables.

George had intended to take a drive, but instead they ended up speaking with Glenn, watching part of the daily exercise.

"Do you mean it?" Glenn asked. "Your father used to get inquiries, but he always turned them away because we had all we could manage."

George grinned. "You start putting the word out about the horses and the boarding. We have room now, and we'll have more as some of the string are sold. You and I can build up this business together." God, he loved the sound of that. "Alan and I need to head back, but I'm serious. This will work out for all of us."

"And my grandson? He loves working with the horses here."

George pushed away from the fence. "Once I get everything together, I'll develop a plan and projections, and we can go over all of it together. I want you and your family to be part of this estate for as long as you wish to stay." They shook hands, and Alan held back a few seconds. George saw Glenn pat him on the shoulder.

"It's good to see him excited," Glenn said, and Alan hurried back inside.

George took off his boots and went right to the small library, where he sat at his worktable and wrote himself notes on everything that he and Alan had talked about. The drawings had been placed on the library table, and Alan wandered over.

"So you have sheep, which can probably be made more profitable. The stables can be made to generate income. The house already does in tourist season." He turned one of the pages and brought it over, then set it on top of where George was writing.

"That's a copy of the garden plans. Mother found them up in one of the attics and had copies made. The originals are in the main library now."

Alan pointed. "What was the plan for all this?"

"Parts of it were accomplished, and some of it never came to be." George set his notes aside. "This part was done, but it grew over some time ago, and my father simply pulled it out, and it's now lawn." George leaned closer. "This part of the gardens is largely intact. The trees were planted, but the folly was never constructed." He went to the large library and pulled open the curtains. "It's supposed to be up on top of that slight rise. But it never got built."

Alan showed him yet another drawing. "Look at that. It's a circular building."

"A folly," George supplied.

"Yeah. And it's supposed to be big. That's your outdoor wedding and party space." Alan grinned at him. "You'd probably need to enlarge it a little with a tent in back, but it would be stunning, complete the garden, and if it were designed right...."

George leapt at Alan and kissed him hard. "Damn. You're here one day and I already feel better about all this, and I think I can actually make it work. The estate has felt like a weight since Dad died, and now...." He swallowed. "I think I can see some sort of light."

CHAPTER 13

ALAN KNEW Justine, George's mother, didn't like him. That was pretty clear from the way she glared at him across the lunch table. He knew that she'd pretty much barged in like she owned the place, the way she had every few days since Alan arrived a week ago. His first plan of attack had been trying to kill her with kindness, but that wasn't working. He thanked Alistair as he sat down, and tried to ignore her glares.

"Where's my son?"

"Working on a couple of deals." George had been working to sell some of the horses he no longer needed, and things on that front were going well. One of his brother's friends was after three of the remaining polo ponies and had been interested in bringing the rest of his string to the estate for Glenn to train. George had been working out the details and logistics when Alan had excused himself.

She cleared her throat daintily. "Don't you have a ranch or something that needs you?" she asked in that snooty way she had whenever she deigned to speak to him.

"My mother is more than capable of running the ranch." The last time he spoke with her, she seemed happy to be back in the saddle and filled with plans for the spring. In truth, Alan was starting to feel like he didn't have a place there any longer. A ranch didn't need two bosses, and with his mother stepping up, that left him wondering what he was going to do. "And George and I...."

"His Grace," Justine muttered as though she were correcting him.

Alan paused. "George and I have been working a lot together."

"But don't you need to go home?" she pressed.

Alan set down his fork. "What's got such a bee in your bonnet?" he asked brusquely. "That George might like me? Is it because I'm a cowboy? American? Or are you one of those delusional people who thinks your son will meet the right girl?" She winced, and Alan had his answer. "I love George, and if I could, I would have asked him to stay with us in Wyoming. Lord knows I wanted him to. My brother and mother think he's pretty amazing too. So my family have welcomed George, which is more than I can say his has done." He picked up his fork again.

"George has to have an heir, and he isn't going to get one with you," she spat.

Alan rolled his eyes. "In case you haven't figured it out, George is a man who is perfectly capable of making up his own mind."

"He ran away for months, and once I get him here and finally settled in his job, you show up."

Alan remained calm. "George knows his duty, ma'am, and he knows what he has to do. It's why he came back here in the first place. But you acting the way you are isn't helping. See, we have a saying back home. You're either part of the solution or part of the problem." He left it at that and took a bite of chicken as George strode in. They shared a smile, and George came right over and kissed him hard in front of his mother, delight dancing in his eyes. All Alan's attention centered on George, and he didn't see how Justine reacted, not that he really cared at this point. After spending the days and nights with George for the past week, he had most definitely fallen under his duke's spell.

A throat clearing parted them, but George practically beamed. "I wanted to talk to you," his mother said haughtily.

"What is it now?" he asked as he sat down next to Alan. George had sent most of his staff over to help his mother settle in, and Alan had seen the house. It was still grand, by his scale. "You have an income of your own, and you are going to have to live within it. The staff here all have jobs, and they helped you out, but they are needed to get the house ready for the upcoming season."

She cleared her throat. "I wanted to talk about your future and that of the estate."

George groaned. "My future is mine to figure out. This house, the estate and title, all of it landed in my lap, and I'm doing my best to figure out how to carry it all into the future. Your meddling isn't helping. And as for your Victorian views on how I should live my life, keep them to yourself. If you can't support what I'm doing and who I am, then I really don't need you. You have a house, and you are welcome to get a job or do other things to occupy your time. But I won't have you sticking your nose where it does not belong." George took Alan's hand. "I love this man. I fell in love with him back in Wyoming, and damn it all, I'm hoping I can convince him to stay here with me."

"But...," she stammered, looking lost.

George leaned over the table. "In one week, Alan and I have figured out how to make the stables pay rather than drain resources. We have a plan to improve the visitor experience with additions to the gift shop. That will take some time, but it will happen. We're looking at possibly letting the house or gardens for parties if I can find a caterer we can work with. It will be one thing at a time. This afternoon, we're going to the various holdings. I want to see the state of things. From there... well, we'll figure it out." He held Alan's hand more tightly, and Alan realized just how much this place was pulling out of George. His fingers quivered. George was strong, but that strength had limits, like everyone else's, and George was coming to his limit. Dealing with his mother was taking all George had.

She stood. "Well, I won't have it," she announced, tossing her napkin on the table.

"You don't get a say." George's arm practically shook while the rest of him remained calm. "This is my life, and you can be part of the solution or the problem." George released his hand. "Mother, this is a huge job," he said more softly. "And I can't do it alone. I'm going to need support."

"But it should be me," she said. "I worked with your father for years."

"I know. But things aren't the same, and they can't be. I have to be free to live my life as I see fit and so I can be happy. Alan makes me happier than I ever thought possible." He turned to him, his expression so gentle. "Alan, I'm just going to ask. I know you're a cowboy and all, but I want you to stay. If I could, I'd trade all this for the biggest ranch I could get so you could run cattle for days, and when it snowed and the power went out, we could cuddle together on the sofa surrounded by dogs."

Alan stood and cupped his cheeks. "I know. But see, something changed for me too. When you left, that ranch just wasn't the same. I wasn't the same. You made me want more than I thought I could have."

"This is all well and good, but what about an heir?" George's mother interjected.

Alan grinned. "You know, I think I'd love a little boy running around this place, one with your eyes. We can look at surrogacy so you can have a kid, or lots of kids. You could teach them how to ride, and I could show them how to bust cattle." Alan tugged George to him. Neither of them paid any attention as George's mother left the room. Alan didn't know if she just stepped out or went home. Either was fine. He only had eyes for George.

"Are you really willing to move here with me? You won't resent me for taking you away?" George asked.

"I can bear to lose a lot of things, but the one thing I've come to realize that I need as much as air and water is you," Alan said, swallowing around the lump in his throat. "I'll figure out a place here. Maybe I'll take charge of livestock planning and management. I understand land and how to take proper care of it."

George practically fell into his arms. "Are you sure this is what you want? That you can be happy here?"

Alan nodded. "You make me happy, and I can't ask for any more than that." He kissed him, holding George tightly. He could be happy here or in Wyoming. Being content and at home wasn't a matter of their location. It was a matter of Alan being where his heart was, and Alan knew his heart was in the hands of his duke, and he wouldn't have it any other way.

EPILOGUE

ALAN HURRIED down the stairs and into the hall, through the small library, and into the large room that he had come to love and had pretty much claimed as his own. George worked in the smaller room, but Alan loved the big space. In going through the attics, they had discovered a ten-foot-long library table from the Victorian period that had been in need of some love. Alan had lovingly repaired and restored it, with the help of a man from the village. Barty had a gift for woodworking as well as horses, and they had returned the hand-carved masterpiece to a place of glory. It was where they kept their master drawing and plans for the estate laid out so they didn't lose sight of their goals. It had been Alan's idea to display them so tourists could see their plans.

Alan paused when he saw George. "The house opens in an hour. I just needed that copy of the garden plan."

"You never stop," George told him with a smile. Spring had come, and the gardens of Blecham Park were filled with shades of green and the occasional red. "And you know your family is arriving this afternoon." He and George had flown back the previous Christmas to visit and to arrange to have Centauri transported to their stables. It was then that they had been introduced to Claude. He was a cattleman himself. Alan's mother apparently met him at a meeting in Cheyenne, and things had bloomed from there.

"I know, and we have dinner with your mother tomorrow," he said softly. In truth, he was so excited about seeing Mom and Chip, he wanted to jump out of his skin. He had kept himself busy so he didn't watch the clock. He also dreaded that dinner, but he didn't see a way out of it. Not that his mom and Chip couldn't handle Justine. "And Mom is apparently bringing Claude with her." He rolled up the drawing he needed and ran it through his hand. "I suspect she's going to announce that they're getting married."

George encircled him in his arms. "How do you feel about that?"

Alan shrugged. "He makes her happy. We saw that at Christmas, and that's all that matters." He was certain of that.

"Then what are you worried about?" George asked. "Is it the ranch?"

"It's all I have left of my father," Alan said softly. "And I always thought my family would be on that land forever. But Claude's place is ten thousand acres, and he runs a large herd. He and Mama will probably live there." He swallowed hard. Alan had no regrets about coming to live here, but that was one thing that was hard for him to swallow.

"Why don't you cross that bridge when you come to it?" George offered gently.

Alan knew he was right. He grinned and thought about chucking his plans for the next few hours, taking George upstairs, and working out some of his frustration in their bedroom, which was most definitely not on the tour. But a throat clearing behind him nixed that idea.

"Yes, Alistair?" George said, and then he backed away.

"We have that special tour in ten minutes," he said, and Alan held George's hand.

"Then we need to get out of here so they can have everything ready. I'm going out to count trees."

George gasped. "What?"

"Well, we have the original garden plans. I want to see what's still there, what doesn't belong, and what we'll need to plant. Then we'll know the scope of the job to return that portion of the garden to the historic design." He grinned. "Wanna come? We can make out under one of the trees when no one's looking." Alan knew that would be more than enough enticement, and he led George out the front door and onto the expansive lawn. Alan didn't release George's hand as they passed the group waiting just outside.

"You're so naughty," George whispered as Alan greeted them with a tip of his cowboy hat, paying no attention to the whispers that went through the group. They continued out into the center of the lawn.

"Hey, everyone knows about us, and I just made their day. Now, let's see what's there and what we need to do." He spread out the drawing, and George moved in close to him. "You know, if you keep doing that, we will never get anything done."

"What?" George asked, and Alan stole a kiss. "Oh, that." He smiled as their gazes locked. "You know we have an audience, and you were the one who wanted to do this."

Alan backed away. Using the house as a reference, he followed the design around to the trees and plantings. The number of trees still there and growing surprised Alan. After marking the ones still in place, they made notes of those that didn't belong and ones that could be replanted. Alan loved being outdoors, and while he had never seen himself as a landscaper, this project was close to his heart.

"Why is this so important to you?" George asked once they made it around the entire section of landscape.

Alan finished making his notes and closed his book. "Because of all the things you and I can do here, this is the one that will have the most lasting impact." He pointed. "That tree there. It's been in that same place for a hundred and fifty years. It's seen how many generations of your family in this house? So many garden parties, wars, peace, all of it. That tree there has seen less, and it doesn't belong. So we'll remove it and plant...." He pointed to the plan. "That tree and that one in its place. They'll be smaller, but we'll nurture them, and in fifty years, when you and I are old and can barely walk, we can look out those library windows and know that our children and our children's children will play under them or take shelter from the rain."

George nodded and slipped his arm around his waist. "I see that. Let's make a list, talk over the changes we want to make, and then we can take them to the planning council for approval. Maybe they'll want to help us."

"Maybe. But the tree planting I'm going to do myself."

George chuckled. "Of course you are. Just let me know when you're going to take your shirt off. I'll sell tickets, and we'll make a fortune." He rolled up the garden plans and took Alan by the hand. "I think we're done, and you promised a make-out session under the trees."

Alan chuckled and followed George into the shade.

Alan tugged George to him under a massive oak tree. "I do love you," Alan whispered.

George took his lips, and Alan held him tightly. "Do you regret anything?"

Alan shook his head. "I'm happy here."

"But my mother... the ranch...," George asked, biting his lower lip.

"If putting up with your mother and a little worry about what will happen to the ranch back home is the price I have to pay to be with you, then I'll gladly pay the toll ten times over. Because, duke of my heart, you are worth it."

"Are you sure?" George asked.

Alan moved them away from the tree. "I was going to do this once my family arrived, but I think this is the perfect place." He turned to where the house sprouted out of the landscape. "This isn't the place where we met, but it is where we will spend the rest of our lives. I know that in my heart." He slowly went down on one knee. "I don't have a ring or anything. I'm just a poor rancher, but what I can offer is my heart, my soul, and my life... forever." He gazed into George's eyes. "Will you marry me?"

George swallowed, and his eyes filled. "Yes," he answered in a whisper.

Alan jumped to his feet, hugged George, and spun him around.

"But you know that no title comes along with it."

Alan drew closer, nearly losing himself in George's eyes, his lips just inches away. "That's fine. You can be the duke of my heart, and I'll be the duke's cowboy. That's all I could ever want."

Keep Reading for an Excerpt from
The Viscount's Rancher
By Andrew Grey

CHAPTER 1

COLLIN STRODE across the late-regency-era stableyard to where his old school chum and friend, George, waited in the archway that led out to the rolling green of his estate. George was the master of all he surveyed, and Collin envied him. He wasn't *jealous*—no mean, backstabbing green-eyed monster—but he wished he was as *happy* as George.

"I love this view," George said just as his partner and soon-to-be husband burst out of the tree line and raced like the wind across the land, long hair bouncing with each stride of his horse. The envy strengthened as Alan continued his ride, back straight, head up and forward, like he was meant to control the beast he rode and anything or anyone who crossed his path.

"What's not to love?" Collin agreed, his gaze following Alan as he made a turn, the horse slowing as they approached. Alan's eyes were wide, his mouth split in a grin. He looked completely out of place surrounded by the other riders in English riding boots, leggings, and helmets. Alan wore jeans and chaps, a flannel shirt, and tooled cowboy boots that were unlike anyone else's in the area. The truth of it was that Alan was unlike anyone Collin had ever met. He was 100 percent his own man and he didn't give a damn what anyone thought, and that made him all the more attractive.

Of course, Collin would never give serious consideration to his fascination with the stunning cowboy. Collin didn't poach, and certainly not from a close friend.

Besides, Alan only had eyes for George.

Alan dismounted the black horse before bounding over and encircling George in his long arms, hugging him hard. It was a very un-English thing to do, and a very Alan spectacle that reminded Collin just how alone he was. The truth was, he wanted someone who would love him as much as Alan clearly adored George. There was no disguising that love, and Alan didn't try. The love the cowboy had for his duke was apparent to everyone who saw them together for more than ten seconds.

"The horse, how is he?" Collin asked, hoping his voice didn't break.

Alan backed away, still smiling as he handed the reins to Collin. "I have no idea what your father is thinking," he answered, his gaze suddenly all business. "He really wants to sell?"

Collin sighed and nodded. "He says he'll never work for polo, and that's what he wanted him for. Not that Jester here is actually his horse. He's mine, officially, but the stable is my father's, so...." Sometimes Collin wished his sire, the Earl of Doddington, would simply stop being a complete controlling wanker.

"He's a fool, and so are you if you sell him," Alan said. "This boy was born to run. It's in his blood, even if it's not in his bloodline. It's what he wants. So if you don't want to sell him, then we'll make a place for him here and we can put him into training as a racer with Centauri. He has the drive and the strength. You saw him; he went like the wind. And let me tell you, he didn't want to stop." Alan was dead serious.

"It *would* get under the old man's skin if I actually raced him and won." The thought delighted him.

Alan chuckled. "Don't get ahead of yourself, but I'd say he definitely has potential."

Glenn, one of the horse wranglers, approached and spoke with Alan briefly before leading Jester away.

"He'll take good care of him."

"Thank you," Collin said. "I knew you'd have some sort of answer. I didn't want to sell him. He was a gift from my uncle."

Alan nodded as though he knew the story. Collin's mother's brother, Uncle Reginald, had given him Jester as a colt two years ago. Reginald died of cancer two months later. Collin's father had hated Uncle Reginald with a passion, though Collin had no idea why, so it didn't take much thought to determine why his father wanted Jester gone. Alan usually tried to keep him out of Collin's father's sight.

"We understand," George said. "Come on. It's getting cold, and with this constant drizzle, I could use something hot." Alan bumped his hip. "To *drink*," George emphasized wickedly. "Come on. Let's go in." He led the way to the Rover, and Alan got behind the wheel. Collin braced himself, because every time George let Alan drive, Collin wondered if he was going to remember to use the left side of the road.

Alan had a tendency to take his half out of the middle. It was fine on the estate, because everyone watched out for him, but on the roads....

"Don't worry. I've got driving on the wrong side the road down now," Alan quipped.

"Sure you do, big guy," Collin teased, and Alan turned to flash him a grin before starting the engine and driving sedately—on the correct side the road—all the way up to the great house. He parked the car, and they went in the private entrance and through to the family apartments, which were closed to the touring public.

"The estate is open today," Alan explained. "George will go down at some point to say hello." He closed the door, his boots clomping on the stone floor until he took them off. They climbed the familiar stairs to a comfortable sitting room in the south wing on the second floor.

"What can I get you?" Alan asked. "I can call down for coffee or tea."

"That would be nice," Collin said. He didn't feel like anything stronger. Alan sent a text message before sitting down. "Thank you for looking at Jester."

Alan grinned. "Are you kidding? I'm going to work with him myself. I've wanted a horse with his unbridled need for speed." He actually rubbed his hands together. "This is going to be great."

George shook his head. "Would you go on down and get the tea? The staff are probably overwhelmed with the guests in the house. I could also use some biscuits and maybe a scone with my tea."

"All right." Alan jumped back up and gave George a kiss before leaving the room.

"You can sure tell he wasn't raised English," Collin said.

"No. He's brash and bold and—"

"Totally amazing. Don't get me wrong for a second. I like that about him. He knows what he wants, and he goes for it without pretense or the need to parse the meaning from what he isn't saying." Collin sighed. "It makes Alan pretty special."

George leaned forward. "When they made Alan, they broke the mold." He smiled happily.

"I can tell. But I'm so tired of dating guys who find out I have a title and decide to see what they can get."

George laughed. "Like Berty?"

"You had to bring him up, didn't you?" Collin said. "I thought he was a nice guy...."

"Until you found out about his wife, two kids, and house in Leeds." George was having way too much fun.

"And let's not forget the two dogs." He shook his head. "And that's not the worst. The last man I got serious with was into latex and everything that goes with it. Now, I'm fine with whatever kink turns someone on, but don't wait until I'm naked, waiting for a guy to join me, only for him to come out in head-to-toe body latex to spring it on me." He closed his eyes. "I want a real man and not someone who knows me as the Viscount Haferton or the heir to the Earl of Doddington. All I get then are fakes and suck-ups."

"That can happen. But there are solid men out there too."

"I know. They just don't seem to cross my path."

"Then come to America with George and me," Alan said as he strode into the room with a tray. He set it on the table and sat back down. "He and I are going back to see my family for a few weeks. Mom needs some help, and I want to spend a little time at home. Mom is getting married in a few months and there's a lot for her to do, but Claude, her fiancé, is going to be traveling on business. I can introduce you around town as a friend from England. No one needs to know your title, and frankly, most people there don't care about that sort of thing. They measure a man by his actions." Alan slipped an arm around George. "That's what drew me to him. He's a good man."

"It just took you some time to see it," George added. "And yeah, you should come with us. We leave in two weeks, so there's time to get a plane ticket."

"There's room at the ranch," Alan said, "but it's a working spread."

"Collin works hard—always has," George said.

"I've been around horses and livestock all my life," Collin told Alan, excited at the prospect of getting away for a while.

Alan leaned forward. "What is your father going to say about you leaving with us for a few weeks?" It was common knowledge that though Collin was close friends with George and Alan, his father didn't like either of them. George and Alan had moved their estate forward and were on the road to profitability, while Collin's father insisted on doing things the way they had been done for years. Fortunately the family had more resources than their land holdings. But Collin's father hadn't kept up with things the way he should have, and the fact that George and Alan had their home set up as a showpiece with a garden restoration in progress and more and more tourists paying them a visit, well, it galled him. In Collin's opinion, his dad wasn't especially ambitious and spent his time being jealous of others rather than doing something to improve his lot. "You know he's going to be as stubborn as a mule."

"Then I'll have to deal with him."

Alan poured George and Collin each a cup of tea and then some coffee for himself. For a Yank, Alan made a nice cup of tea. As he sipped it, Collin tried to figure out what the hell he was going to do about dear old Dad.

"YOU AREN'T going anywhere. I need you here looking after our horses instead of running off on some holiday with the duke," Collin's father declared his study. He had a book in one hand and a glass of whisky in the other, which would have been fine if it hadn't been two in the afternoon when everyone else was working. Not Dad. He thought of himself as a man of leisure. More like a lazy ass, in Collin's opinion, which he kept to himself.

"I haven't had any time away from the estate in years. I work hard, and you know it." Harder than his father, but Collin held his tongue. "I have money of my own. I'm not asking you to pay for anything." That was something else his father didn't like. When his mother had passed two years ago, she had left everything—no inconsiderable amount— to Collin. His father had been trying to get his hands on it for some time, but Collin and his solicitor had the money tied up tight and well away from his father. "I'm an adult, and I don't need your permission to go."

His father set his book aside, and the whisky in his glass sloshed as he sat forward. "Now listen here, boy. You need to think about how you're going to continue this family. That title of yours is secondary to mine and doesn't come with anything. The earldom, my title, is attached to this estate, and it needs to continue after I'm through. You need to make sure it passes to your heirs as well. Wait." He sneered. "Your kind and those over at the dukedom don't have heirs."

Collin remained standing, hating the way his father dismissed him and his friends. "Why do you act like this?" He decided to try the direct approach. "You know the duke and his husband are good people. They helped you out last fall, and yet you talk that way."

"People like that—" his father began.

"Like what? Hard workers? People who are willing to put in the effort?" Collin met his father's steely gaze, expecting a blowup. "You should be ashamed of how you talk about them and about me. I'm your son."

His father glared at him. "There are times I wonder about that."

Collin could feel the heat rising in his cheeks. "Really? You're saying that Mom had an affair? Really? And she found someone as pale and round-faced as you are to screw around with?" He'd always wondered why his mother had stayed with his father. The man had few redeeming qualities.

"I just meant…," he blustered, and for a second Collin thought he might have seen the first hint that his father knew he'd gone too far— something rare in the man.

"I know what you were saying. That I don't measure up and that you wanted someone different for a son. Maybe you wanted someone who was straight, or maybe a kid who is as useless and lazy as you." He had had enough of his father's picking, controlling attitude. "I'll leave in two weeks and will be away for a fortnight. I have a right, and I'm perfectly free to go."

"Fine," his father snapped. "But I expect something in return."

Collin chuckled. "Like what? You forget that I don't owe you anything. My title has been registered with Debrett's, so trying to remove it would cause talk. In fact, anything you do will cause talk, and I know you don't want that." His father wasn't exactly in favor with any of the local gentry, so a scandal would only push him further to the edges of local society, and that would hurt. "Just stop, Father. You don't get to control me or run my life."

To Collin's surprise, his father picked up his book once more and just shook his head. "Fine. You go to America with your friends." The way he said it made Collin wonder what he thought he was up to. But Collin wasn't going to stick around to try to puzzle out the many wavering paths of his father's mind. That was a job that would stymie a team of psychoanalysts.

"I'll make sure everything is seen to and let you know the exact dates I'll be gone." He left the room and then placed a call to George, who made flight arrangements for him, and Collin was all set. He hung up the phone and wondered why he was so excited. He had just volunteered to go to America and spend two weeks on a ranch. Yes, he worked with horses, but he knew very little about being a cowboy.

Still, it was a chance to get away from his father and Westworth and all the problems his father seemed intent on ignoring. Perhaps with him gone, the earl would have to get up off his posterior and do something. Collin still wondered what his father had up his sleeve, but he put the thoughts aside.

His phone rang, and Collin answered it right away. "What's up?" he asked Riley, his best friend from school.

"I was calling to see if you wanted to hit the pub tonight." Riley always had enough energy for three people. His mother worked on George's estate and had since Riley was a kid. Riley was whip-smart, and George's father had helped him get into some of the best schools, which was where Collin had met him.

"Sure. I can meet you." He checked the time. "Hook and Castle in an hour?"

"Sounds good," Riley said just as Collin's father entered the room. He fixed Collin with a glare. He didn't like Riley either. Collin was starting to think his father hated everyone in Collin's life. Not that it mattered.

"Yes, it does," he said gently. "I'll meet you at the pub, and I can tell you all about my upcoming trip to America." He held his father's gaze, watching that little vein on his forehead.

"You're leaving?" Riley asked, aghast.

"Just for two weeks. I'm traveling with the duke and Alan, and I'll be spending the time on a ranch there." He waited until his father left the room again before smiling.

"I take it that little scene was for your father. Are you really going?" Riley knew the workings of his relationship with his father better than Collin did sometimes.

"Yeah. I think it's time I try to build a life of my own somehow, and I'm not going to do it here. My father is getting even worse."

"The gay thing?" Riley asked.

"And that 'carry on the family line' thing," he added. "I'm tired of all of it. Enough is enough, so I'm leaving the country for a while."

Riley sighed. "I wish I could go. I'd love to find me a cowboy and ride him over the range." Collin snickered at Riley's joke. Or maybe he was serious. It was sometimes hard to tell. "I'll still be here trying to get this spirit shop of mine up and running, and you'll be over in America finding cowboys to ride."

Collin should be so lucky.

Scan the QR Code
Below to Order!

ANDREW GREY is the author of more than two hundred works of Contemporary Gay Romantic fiction, including an Amazon Editors Best Romance of 2023. After twenty-seven years in corporate America, he has now settled down in Central Pennsylvania with his husband of more than twenty-five years, Dominic, and his laptop. An interesting ménage. Andrew grew up in western Michigan with a father who loved to tell stories and a mother who loved to read them. Since then he has lived throughout the country and traveled throughout the world. He is a recipient of the RWA Centennial Award, has a master's degree from the University of Wisconsin–Milwaukee, and now writes full-time. Andrew's hobbies include collecting antiques, gardening, and leaving his dirty dishes anywhere but in the sink (particularly when writing). He considers himself blessed with an accepting family, fantastic friends, and the world's most supportive and loving partner. Andrew currently lives in beautiful, historic Carlisle, Pennsylvania.

Email:andrewgrey@comcast.net

Website:www.andrewgreybooks.com

Follow me on BookBub

Emmett McElroy is the cowboy horses hate. When his heir apparent brother dies and his father has a heart attack, he does his duty and steps up as head of the family ranch, but he wishes things were different and his life choices were his own. Just when he begins to get his legs under him, he arrives home to find his high school crush has been hired as ranch foreman.

Ex-rodeo cowboy Nathaniel Zachary desperately needs work. When Mrs. McElroy offers him a job while her husband recovers, he jumps at it. The only issue is Emmett... because Nathaniel has never been able to get his best friend's brother out of his mind.

Tensions only increase when, after drowning his sorrows, Emmett foolishly agrees to enter a bucking bronc contest at the local rodeo. The attraction that grows as Nathaniel helps prepare Emmett for the contest is something neither of them expected, but as Emmett's father's health improves, the happiness they've built may break faster than a cowboy thrown from the meanest bronc.

Scan the QR Code
Below to Order!

Rafe Carrera hasn't seen his Uncle Mack since he was a kid, so when he inherits his ranch, it throws him like a bucking horse. He's been on his own for a long time. Now suddenly everyone wants to be his friend... or at least get friendly enough to have a chance in buying the ranch.

Russell Banion's family may own a mega-ranch in Telluride, but Russell made his own way developing software. He misses his friend Mack, and purchasing the ranch will help him preserve Mack's legacy—and protect his own interests. It's a win-win. Besides, spending time with Rafe, trying to soften him up, isn't exactly a hardship. Soon Russell realizes he'll be more upset if Rafe does decide to leave.

But Rafe isn't sure he wants to sell. To others in the valley, his land is worth more than just dollars and cents, and they'll do anything to get it. With Russell's support, Rafe will have to decide if some things—like real friendship, neighborliness, and even love—mean more than money.

SCAN THE QR CODE
BELOW TO ORDER!

ANDREW GREY

Two cowboys.
Twenty years together.
One chance to save their love.

SECOND GO-ROUND

Former world champion bronco rider Dustin and rancher Marshall have been life partners for more than twenty years, and time has taken its toll. Their sex life is as dusty as the rodeo ring. Somehow their marriage hasn't turned out how they planned.

But when a new family moves in up the road with two young boys, one very sick, Dustin and Marshall realize how deep their ruts are and that there might be hope to break them. After all, where they're from, the most important part of being a man is helping those who need it.

A new common purpose helps break down the deep routines they've fallen into and makes them realize the life they've been living has left them both cold and hollow. Spending time with the kids—teaching them how to be cowboys—reignites something they thought lost long ago. But twenty years is a lot of time to make up for. Can they find their way back to each other, or are the ruts they've created worn too deep?

Scan the QR Code
Below to Order!

Half a Cowboy

Andrew Grey

Ever since his discharge from the military, injured veteran Ashton Covert has been running his family ranch—and running himself into the ground to prove he still can.

Ben Malton knows about running too. When he takes refuge in Ashton's barn after an accident in a Wyoming blizzard, he's thinking only of survival and escaping his abusive criminal ex, Dallas.

Ashton has never met a responsibility he wouldn't try to shoulder. When he finds Ben half-frozen, he takes it upon himself to help. But deadly trouble follows Ben wherever he goes. He needs to continue on, except it may already be too late.

Working together brings Ben and Ashton close, kindling fires not even the Wyoming winter can douse. Something about Ben makes Ashton feel whole again. But before they can ride into the sunset together, they need to put an end to Dallas's threats. Ben can make a stand, with Ashton's help—only it turns out the real danger could be much closer to home.

SCAN THE QR CODE
BELOW TO ORDER!

HARD
ROAD

Back

ANDREW GREY

Rancher Martin Jamuson has a deep understanding of horses. He just wishes his instincts extended to his best friend, Scarborough Croughton, and the changes in their feelings toward each other. Martin may be the only friend Scarborough has in their small town, but Scarborough is a man of secrets, an outsider who's made his own way and believes he can only rely on himself when the chips are down. Still, when he needs help with a horse, he naturally comes to Martin.

As they work together, Martin becomes more determined than ever to show Scarborough he's someone he can trust… maybe someone he can love. Even if it risks their friendship, both men know the possibility for more between them deserves to be explored. But when Scarborough's past reemerges, it threatens his home, horses, career, and even their lives. If they hope to survive the road before them, they'll have to walk it together… and maybe make the leap from cautious friends to lovers along the way.

SCAN THE QR CODE
BELOW TO ORDER!

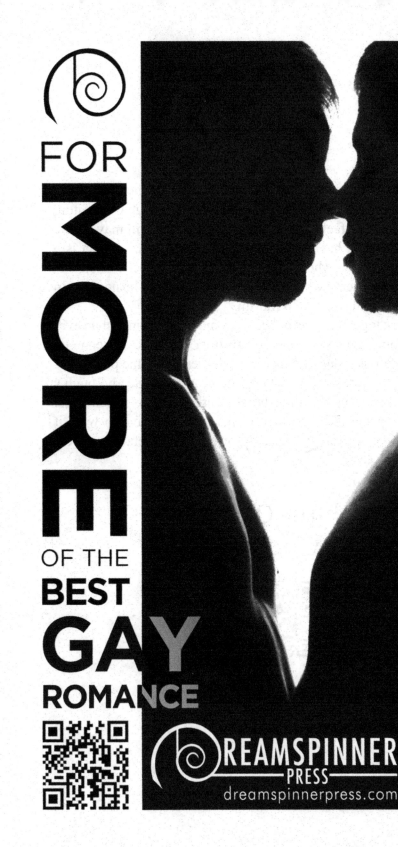